Promise

of

Tomorrow

Mark Miller

MillerWords
PO Box 1622
Mount Dora, FL 32756

Second Edition

For discounts on bulk purchases, please contact MillerWords Educational Sales at **Sales@MillerWords.com**

Printed in the United States of America

2 4 6 8 10 9 7 5 3

Library of Congress Control Number: 2016909872

ISBN: 978-0692740743

One

Salvation

The story of faith is as everlasting as the wind and stars. It is the story that breaks families and binds them. It is the search for truth. It is past, future and present.

It is the story of the Umble family.

Luke Umble trusted his faith, but he considered himself a practical man. That made the decision to leave difficult, not only for him, but for his wife, children and parents. Luke did not always agree with his father, but the decision had to be made. The story of fathers and sons, another of the eternal tales.

Luke snapped the reigns and the tired horse pressed forward against the coming windstorm. The weather grew so bad this summer that a sunny day seemed a rarity. The lack of rain dried every inch of ground. Dry dirt cut like tiny slivers of glass in the relentless wind. Small cyclones whipped up on wide fields once occupied by corn and wheat.

Luke's *Englische* friends spoke of this change in weather over the past several years. The Amish made no special preparations. They said it was all part of God's plan. Besides, who would rely on technology to predict weather? For all they knew, the technology caused it. Cars carelessly burned the fuel so heartlessly ripped from the Earth by massive oilrigs. Closer to home, massive combines and plows chewed up the ground while they showered the crops with poison to kill the insects.

Except, the combines and plows had been silent for months.

This drought spread across the state, the country and, from what Luke could gather, the world. In his youth, Luke fancied travelling the world. He thought, during his *Rumschpringa* that he might go so far as to see the North Pole. He dreamed big and that caused a rift between him and his father. All in all, it did not matter. The *Englische* said if the drought did not end by December, there would be no more polar ice caps. Those people long threatened a plague called global warming. Maybe, Luke wondered, if it was Old Nick stoking the fires and making room for so many new guests. Even among the Amish, Luke reckoned there would be many going down, not up, when the time came. Too many new converts, his father said.

The horse faltered and the cart jerked to a stop. Luke knew his animal was tired and thirsty. They barely had enough water for the *kinder*. The rivers and wells became unsafe, something about the water table according to the *Englische*. It hurt Luke to treat the animals so poorly. He depended on his horses, cows and other livestock in better times. It felt like a sin to let them down when they depended on him. He reasoned with his wife Annie that a glass of water was better spent on one of their children and they would walk if need be.

Annie found her answer to the situation in prayer. She reminded Luke that God often tested the faithful. She found comfort in their trials now. To her, it meant God was close. The Bible told stories that happened hundreds of years ago. The Lord tested them now, today. When most people panicked, Annie had peace. For too long, she believed the distance between God and man to be increasing. If people believed the rapture was coming, then to her, it meant the Lord was coming with it.

Her wisdom gave Luke strength. Theirs had been an old-fashioned arranged marriage. Until their wedding day, Luke could count on one hand the number of times he had spoken to Annie. That did not mean he did not like her. To the contrary, he fell in love the day they took their nuptials and his feelings only grew stronger with each passing day. Luke's first love was the land. He never took time to seek a companion. His mother forced it on him and he went reluctantly.

Luke admitted that it was the best decision of his life. He did not know he was incomplete until Annie completed him. So many verses from the Bible suddenly made sense to Luke in a new way. One of his favorites came from Proverbs: "He who finds a wife finds a good thing and obtains favor from the Lord." That favor came swiftly and in the form of their children. Not only did they produce five beautiful children, but the Lord also smiled on their farm. Year after year, Luke's crops yielded more than any of his neighbors.

Luke did not dare to think himself favored. He did, however, do one thing different from his brethren. Luke made it a point to give thanks every day and to always accept God's gifts without question, even when he did not understand them. Each of their children was a gift and each came into this world with good health and good sense. As they grew, Luke and Annie noticed a change in their youngest daughter. She did not have the strength of body as their other children did. By the time she turned ten, she was confined to a wheelchair due to what the *Englische* doctors called Muscular Dystrophy. The doctors told them it was an inherited disease, but none of their living family members showed any of the related symptoms. Luke did not understand why his precious Katie had to suffer so, but she learned to cope with the chair over the past several years. He also witnessed in her God's gift of a loving and generous heart. She knew his mind better than any of his other children, not counting baby Matthew, who could not yet speak.

All of their children brought Luke great joy. He strove never to favor one over the other as he never asked favor from the Lord. Luke lived the life he was given, content with all of its gifts and trials. He looked forward to the day that his oldest boy John would take over the farm. With the long coming changes in weather, it now seemed a real possibility that there would be no farm for John to inherit. Now almost nineteen years old, Luke knew his boy would have to choose a path. John delayed his *Rumschpringa* and baptism. This caused some uneasy conversations between Luke, the Bishop and some of the other men. It was not unheard of for a young man to leave the Amish, but it was frowned upon for an unsaved man to live among them.

As independent as John seemed to be, their sixteen-year-old daughter Mary looked to never leave the house. She stayed close to her mother and learned as many skills as she could from Annie. Luke saw much of himself in his daughter. She did not display any interest in finding a husband. Secretly, that settled well with Luke. He believed there was not a young man that he knew that would be good enough for Mary. Secretly, Luke admonished himself for his prideful thoughts.

Where Katie was gentle and calm, Henry made up for it with unusually high energy and curiosity. The boy spent his eighth birthday catching frogs and snakes in a dried up pond. Unfortunately, it was not dry enough and Henry lost both of his shoes in the knee-deep mud. Between Katie and baby Matthew, Annie had more than enough responsibility. Luke took charge of Henry, helping him with schoolwork and washing him in the horse trough when he was too dirty to be allowed in the house.

Luke and Annie found a natural balance in the care and nurturing of their children. Where one parent had a shortcoming, the other had a strength. After a full day's work, they ate dinner as a family and both Luke and Annie spent time with their children, reading scripture or playing games. Most nights ended with the sound of laughter. Only in recent months did their life change.

The *Englische* had warned for years of the worsening environmental conditions. Luke turned to men he thought to be wiser than himself. Those men paid no heed to the outside world, but then they were the first to leave when things went bad. Luke always listened to his father and his father told him to stay put.

"The Lord has a plan for us and that plan is to stay on our land. Our feet were meant for this Earth. We are made from its dust and we shall return to it," said Levi Umble.

Throughout his life, Luke became accustomed to obeying his father. He did so on many occasions without question. After all, the Bible says it should be so. However, Levi did not approve of Luke's marriage to Annie. In their many talks, Levi insisted Luke should keep to the farm and not bother with the distractions and temptations of a woman. Luke believed these thoughts came from his father not being reconciled with God over the loss of Luke's mother shortly before the wedding. After that, Luke's relationship with his father faltered. He loved the man who gave him life, but believed he stumbled on his path.

Twenty years later, Luke now rode on the open bench of his old wagon. He built it by hand and it served him well for many years. He did not like being out in another dust storm. Still, he almost preferred it to his destination. He needed to make it to his father's house. Luke knew this talk would be a confrontation. He knew, right or wrong, that it would be difficult to change his father's mind. Levi intended to stay in his home. Luke had the overwhelming task of convincing him to leave. Even Bishop Kurtz left over a week ago. They had nothing here now and needed to move someplace safe.

Another first stirred in the front of Luke's mind today. First Corinthians told him, "Love bears all things, believes all things, hopes all things, endures all things." He would get through all of this with the love of his wife. He had the love of his family. For Luke, it did not matter where they ended up or where God sent them. As long as they had each other, they would be home. And he gave thanks for that.

Luke urged the starving horse forward. Another gust of wind almost rocked Luke from his seat. The horse lowered its head and whinnied. It did not have the will to continue. Luke guessed he only had maybe one hundred feet to go. To his left, he could make out the wobbling of the split-rail fence marking the barren pasture of his father's farm.

Luke jumped from the bench and pulled the horse toward the fence. He could not see his father's barn through the brown haze, but led the horse in the direction of where it should have been. Ten minutes later, Luke unhitched the horse inside the dark barn. The storm did not seem as bad inside the wooden-framed building. This barn survived more spring storms and winter blizzards than Luke had lived through. He could hear creaking from the high timbers and the loft door banged on its hinges. Somewhere in one of the back stalls, a few chickens clucked. Luke saw no sign of his father's cows. The *Englische* must have come for them already, he assumed.

It only took a few more minutes to remove the harness. "Earl, I'm going to leave you here for a bit. I will come back for you, old friend," Luke said to his horse.

The howling wind dared Luke to take the short walk from the barn to the house. Luke had to push against the forceful wind to open the smooth pine door. He clamped down on his hat and dashed into the fury of dust and debris.

The trip from the barn to the house became a metaphor for his life. If the barn represented birth, then the house was the doorway to salvation. In between, the world became a tumult of events and choices. If he was lucky, God gave Luke a good hundred years on this Earth. Almost half of that passed in a blink. Somehow, he was forty years old. In his mind and heart, he still felt twenty, or maybe younger. He could not quite comprehend how time evaporated in front of him, like the droughts did to their water supply this spring. If he tried to stop time, it would be as futile as trying to catch the dust whipping around him with a net.

Behind him, Luke heard the barn door banging against the frame. He must have missed the latch. Left at the mercy of the wind, it would surely be torn free in no time. Luke decided he had gone too far to go back. The angry gusts of dirt and sand pushed him toward his father's house. The loss of the small side door would not endanger the few animals inside, so Luke left it to God's will. Strange how he could still hear the banging over the howling wind as he climbed the stairs to his father's house.

Luke almost tripped over the old rocking chair. A few of the back spindles broke, probably from tipping over. It needed a new coat of white paint, but it needed that before the severe weather came. Luke slid the chair up against the house. He prayed that it did not get carried away on the wind and cause anybody else some harm. Even before he turned back to the rattling screen door, he watched the chair slide down the porch and crash into the rail. The wind seemed to be growing in intensity with each new day.

Levi Umble kept the hook in place on his screen door all the time. In recent years, he stated he no longer wanted uninvited guests. Many of the other

Amish in their community left their doors and windows unlocked all of the time. Luke's neighbors enjoyed a friendly visit and never turned anyone away. They said they would rather welcome an unexpected guest than not be able to find a friend when they had need. After Luke's mother passed, Levi adapted some of the behaviors of the New Amish.

The converted *Neufremdefreunds* brought their old world mentality with them. They had habits of locking their doors and not always sharing their bounty. These behaviors came from the *Englische* outside, where crime and sinful deeds necessitated such things. The *Neufremdefreunds*, or new friendly strangers, emulated the Amish in hopes of finding salvation. The fact that they remained connected to the internet and still drove cars told Luke that some were not as committed as others. The Umbles and their neighbors tolerated the New Amish in their community. They assumed their intentions to be honorable and not as selfish as they appeared.

Luke pounded on the narrow strip of wood holding the screen in place. He knew his father could not hear him, yet he waited for a response. Another surge of wind ripped Luke's hat from his head. It disappeared in a spiral of grit and straw, off the porch and into the oblivion of dull brown sky. Annie would not be pleased that he lost his second hat this week. Instead of waiting any longer, Luke pulled hard on the curved metal handle. The threads of the eyehook tore loose from the door and Luke could now reach the handle of the solid oak door hidden behind the screen door.

Locked.

"Father!" called Luke. He could barely hear himself over the storm. "Father. Levi Umble, open this door. You knew this day would come. You cannot hide behind your locks."

No response.

Part of Luke's mind imagined his father on the floor of the kitchen, suffering a heart attack. For whatever reason, Luke's mind often did that to him. He could not help picturing the worst of any situation. It happened more with his children, although he knew God had his hand on them. He had no reason to expect such things, but thoughts crept into his head of their own accord. His father could be called different things, but not one of poor health. Maybe the storm heightened his receptiveness to such thoughts, Luke reasoned. A small sense of panic caused him to break the glass pane in the old door. As a boy, Levi would have brought the rod to Luke's backside for that.

The sound of breaking glass and the wail of wind through the new hole must have stirred Levi. Luke found him wrestling his way up from his wide-cushioned chair. Luke got inside and pushed the door closed. The wind streaming in whined like a high note of the flute his daughter Mary played on birthdays and at Christmas.

"Why would you damage a man's property like that?" demanded Levi. The black and gray hairs of his beard twitched as he ground his teeth. Levi looked like he wanted to say more, but chose not to speak.

"If you would not act like a *Neufremdefreund*, it would not have been needed. Have faith that the Lord would not let anyone through your door that might harm you. If he did, then it is His time to call you home," said Luke. He stepped clear of the door and tried to catch his breath. He did not realize the exertion it took struggling through the harsh wind.

"You break into my home and speak to me with an insolent tongue? Are you my son or a temptation from Lucifer? If I taught you anything, I taught you to honor your father," said Levi.

Luke looked at the man, looked down at him. All of his life, he looked up to his father. When he was small, there was a natural height difference, but in his heart, there had always been a greater one. Like most boys, Luke's father always seemed to be about ten feet tall. Then, as decades snuck by, one day Luke noticed that he physically stood taller than the aging, graying man. That did not change Luke's feelings for him. He loved his father and saw him walking tall in the glory of God's light. Only in recent years did Levi start to seem like a small man. Part of it had to do with age, but Luke also felt like Levi strayed from the path. Out of respect, and the sensible urging of his wife, Luke did not say this to his father. That time would come some other day; today had its own matters to tend to.

"I do honor you with all my heart. You are my father and have my every respect. But today is not a day for gentle words or subtle actions. We have spoken on this matter a time or two before. There is no more time for talk. Your decision today means your life or death," said Luke.

Luke dropped onto his father's couch. He felt a little leery putting his back to the pair of windows behind him. He could not see the storm on the other side of the drawn shades, but that would not keep something from smashing through the glass at any moment.

"You and your talk." Levi waved a dismissive hand. Luke could see the expression on his face. It told him that his father had not changed his mind.

"Father, if we do not leave today, I do not think we will have houses to sleep in tomorrow. Besides, this is our last chance to go with the *Englische*," explained Luke.

Levi stood over his son. He said, "It is God's will that we walk apart from the *Englische*. I was born in this house. My mother and your mother are both buried in the cemetery down the road. I intend to be buried with them."

Luke stood and took his father's hand. His emotions swirled like the dust outside. The man's stubbornness made him anger and his ignorance made him sad. He said, "You talk of being apart from the *Englische*, yet you have in your house the trappings of the newly converted. How do you know it is not God's will for us to travel with the outsiders?"

"Bah." Levi pulled away from his son. "I put a lock on my door and you accuse me of losing faith." Levi started moving toward his bedroom. If he closed the door, the conversation would be over and Luke knew he would lose his father.

A horrendous creaking shook the house. A terrible noise of breaking wood came from above them. Luke assumed that a section of shingles had been torn from the roof. As if Luke needed more proof of his argument, breaking glass came from the kitchen. Without looking, he knew the small window above the sink had shattered.

"There will soon be nothing left here. This storm has gotten worse than any of us could have guessed.

Come with me. I fear, if you do not, you will be buried in this room and not down the road."

Levi had a wild look in his eyes. Lately, Luke had only seen tiredness and sadness in his father's face. The rattling, shaking storm must have awoken something else. Maybe a sense of self-preservation. Luke firmly believed that God took people into his arms at their appointed time. That did not mean his father had to lie down and wait for it to happen. None of them had to fall victim to the dust storms because the *Englische* offered to help them. Their way of life was about to change, but he knew they could keep their faith.

"Are you ready to embrace the *Englische* technology?" asked Levi.

"They have made accommodations for us. All of your friends and neighbors are waiting, even the *Neufremdefreunds*. Stop stalling," said Luke.

Levi continued toward his bedroom. The front door rattled on its hinges.

"Where are you going father? You don't have time to pack!"

Levi waved that dismissive hand again. That hand always represented strength to Luke, but now it looked like a weak, confused gesture. Levi disappeared around the corner and reemerged almost immediately with a scuffed, leather suitcase.

Already packed. Luke wanted to grab his father by the shoulders and shake him. He wanted to know why the man put up such a fight if he was already packed. Luke maintained a level head. If he let emotion over take him, it could endanger his entire family.

The father and son made their way to the barn. Levi moved much slower than Luke would have liked and the wind picked up considerably in the short time he was in his father's house. At least they did not have to struggle with the barn door. Only its hinges remained. The door probably flew somewhere over the back pasture now. In the barn, they did not escape the howling wind as Luke had earlier. Luke planned to ride the wagon to his waiting wife and children. An unmoving horse faltered that plan.

"Oh, Earl," said Luke. He instinctively reached for his hat to remove it as a sign of respect for the recently departed, but his hand found nothing on his head. "He was a good horse. Where are your horses?"

Levi removed his hat and said, "I put them to pasture yesterday. What do we do now?"

"Now?" repeated Luke. "Now we run."

When Luke later described the events of his and his father's escape, he said it was like two tornadoes came together for the worst kind of barn raising. Heavy four by four timbers danced over their heads even before they made it outside. They tried to follow the split rail fence, but it vanished faster than they could move. Luke had traveled between his home and his father's for enough years that he could walk it blindfolded. With the dense clouds scraping the dirt from the ground, essentially they were blindfolded.

Luke prayed, under his breath. His father would not have heard him if he had tried to speak louder. He said, "Father, I ask for your deliverance, not for me, but for my family. I have a responsibility to keep to a good woman and I must continue to teach my children how to share Your glory. The Umbles are about to start a new journey, one which I think will bring us closer to You and each other. Please guide my feet so that I may lead them into Your bosom."

Only by God's grace did Luke and his father reach his waiting family. Annie had been talking with the *Englische* and they sent a vehicle. Luke tossed his father's suitcase into the back with their meager possessions and they piled into the car. The Englische driver did not wait for them to buckle their seatbelts. Luke looked at the scared faces surrounding him: Annie bundled Matthew close, John, Mary and Katie looked at him. Henry watched out the back window. A roaring sound, possibly a hundred times louder than the locomotive that used to pass through the nearby town, came down around them. They all watched as their own house collapsed and the splintered wood whisked up into the sky. The *Englische* driver sped away from the destruction.

The drive did not take that long and the *kinder* remained surprisingly calm. The storm did not seem to follow them, but the sky did not clear either. The vehicle stopped near a chain link fence that wobbled with the occasional gusts. Luke suspected it had been hastily constructed and with little ethic for the finished product. With the windstorms, it would likely not last the day. Nor did it matter.

Climbing out of the wagon-like vehicle, Luke watched two small groups of people, heads down, carrying only a few bags, run through a gate in the temporary fencing. It looked like there should have been a guard present, but perhaps they were past that pretense now. No one else in Luke's family knew what to expect on the other side of that fence. Only he had been in communication with the *Englische*, only he made arrangements for their salvation.

He prayed; Lord knew he prayed. The decision to rely on the *Englische* did not come easy. Ultimately, it came to a choice between living or dying. Luke spoke openly that he did not fear death. Leaving this mortal world would deliver him into the hands of his savior. That is what he said when he spoke often with friends from the church. In his heart, he did not know what to think. The world changed drastically over the past few years. While the Amish faith grew strong and attained a record high membership, the rest of the world seemed to slip into chaos. All the same, Luke wanted his *kinder* to have a chance at their own lives. He was not ready to see life taken from them before they had a chance to live it.

He believed that the *Englische* and their life without value brought the world to the breaking point. It caused his heart to ache that it seemed the *Englische* offered the only salvation. Luke chose to escape with the *Englische* like so many other Amish, in their district and around the world. Because of his indecisiveness, or maybe hope, Luke waited until the last possible day to leave. Now, they had no home to go back to. They could only go forward.

John wrestled Katie's wheelchair from atop the vehicle and unfolded it. Luke could see that it would not roll easy on the sand-covered pavement. He turned his attention to Annie. She held Matthew close to her bosom, keeping the wind and debris out of his face. It saddened Luke that Matthew would never know this world. Once his family clambered out of the vehicle, Luke moved to the rear to unload their bags.

"Leave them. I will take care of them," demanded the driver. "Get your family in there. Another tornado is coming."

Luke trusted the *Englische* driver to keep his word. He nodded thanks and ushered his family toward the gate. A section of the chain link tore free with a gust of wind. The spinning metal whipped over their heads close enough that Luke thought he could feel it touch the tip of his uncovered hair. He thanked God for not making him any taller. Once he got his family to the transport, he conceded that the Lord could do with him as He wished. Until that time, Luke needed to keep his wife and *kinder* safe.

He looked over his shoulder to see his father stumbling after them, one hand on his hat, the other holding his suitcase. It figured that Levi Umble would be so stubborn as not to trust the driver with his bag. Luke had no contract or guarantee for the outcome of the day's events. He only had the word of an *Englische* and he prayed that was good enough.

They passed a few small, temporary-looking buildings. They all looked empty. A video screen flickered on the wall. It scrolled through a few advertisements, mostly for travel products. It seemed that the *Englische* need for consumerism would not cease, even as their world did. Most of the ads were unreadable. One ad from Time Magazine stayed on the screen for a moment. It boasted the release of their final issue with an all-black cover showing the name of the magazine in red and the year, 2057, in a metallic silver. The starkness of it said so much to Luke, but he had very little time to process it. The screen flickered again and then went blank as if electricity no longer flowed to it.

A moment later, the *Englische* driver ran past them. Luke saw that he did not carry a single one of their bags. He wanted to trust the man. He needed to trust the *Englische*. They were about to take responsibility for everything he held dear in this world. Luke looked back to see if he could see why the driver ran from his vehicle. A powerful roar of wind gave Luke the answer.

Luke froze. The sound of the tornado did not come from behind them. It came from the direction they were going. Luke grabbed Annie by the arm, right above the elbow. He slapped his other free hand on John's shoulder. The boy struggled with his sister's wheelchair and stopped without extra urging. Katie did not weigh that much, but the chair was old and second-hand. Luke stared into the brown sky expecting to see the tornado drop down on top of them. His heart raced. Over and over, he repeated to himself, "Not yet, Lord."

Instead of coming closer, the sound seemed to move away from them. With the wild wind, it became difficult to tell anything for certain. Another loud noise rose up behind them. Luke realized the first sound had to be one of the large transports leaving. There would not be many left now. The noise behind them had the unmistakable whine of a twister. It yanked the last of the chain link fence from the ground.

It has been said that the Amish do not know fear. Everything moves according to God's plan. Good or bad, as it occurs, is part of that plan. If it is God's will, then there is nothing to fear. For the first time in his life, Luke Umble felt true fear. Be it Lucifer's strength from a sinful world, or God's wrath wiping that world clean, the storm would not relent.

Luke pushed his family forward. Nothing worked like the *Englische* said. No one met them to take his tickets or guide them to the correct transport. A faceless doll and a white kapp blew past them. Luke led his family in the direction from which the Amish items came. He guessed other Amish had to be that way, although he could not see them.

Out of the dust, a low rectangular shape took form. It reminded Luke of big metal shipping crates. They received food donations delivered on large trucks in tanks like these last winter. He also thought they used them to ship goods over the ocean. Inside, Luke could make out a few familiar faces. At least one of the families had been neighbors of theirs. Luke shoved his father inside and then turned to help John lift Katie and her chair over the threshold. Luke hurriedly counted his family members. Without asking if everyone made it, two *Englische* slammed the heavy metal doors closed. A hissing noise followed that made Luke think they were sucking the air out of the crowded room.

They had nowhere to sit. Bodies pressed against bodies. Luke felt like he could not breathe. He realized that the *Englische* did not suck out the air. Instead, the gritty, warm air had been replaced by a cool, filtered air. The soothing temperature helped him relax momentarily. Then the crate rocked from side to side. The transport shook with a thunderous sound. The tornado had to be right on top of them.

The transport lurched. An Amish man, that Luke did not recognize, fell against Annie and the baby. He apologized and stood up as best he could. The transport lurched again. Then it felt as if they tumbled upside down. Luke saw beards curl and women's long hair raise up from under their kapps. His feet never left the floor, but his stomach turned worse than the time

Earl accidentally kicked him when they were changing his horseshoes.

The thought of leaving his trusted horse behind in his father's barn left Luke feeling guilty. He knew that the drought and the toxins caused the horse's death. That did not make him feel any less responsible. Luke witnessed Earl's birth and together they worked the land for over fifteen years. Of all the things they left behind, including their abandoned necessities, Luke knew he would miss Earl the most.

The transport shook again. Luke wondered if it would come apart as the wind buffeted it. No one spoke. Luke could hear a few whimpers and moans from the other passengers. His own infant son made no noise, coddled in his mother's arms. Someone in the back corner recited the Hail Mary.

Luke took a deep breath. He did not realize how frayed his nerves were. The tension had been growing for weeks as more of their neighbors left. Finally, it came to the day where he had to force his father out of his house. From the way things looked as those *Englische* closed the doors, they could not have waited any later. Luke silently joined that unknown voice in prayer.

After a few more minutes, the shaking and shuddering stopped. Luke did not think the people in the transport could not have been quieter. Now, silence seemed to swell inside the cramped room. The refugees collectively held their breath. None of them had ever experienced anything like this day brought them. According to the *Englische*, Luke expected their trip to take less than one half of an hour. Unlike the man that failed to bring their luggage, the *Englische* that explained the plan to Luke seemed to be accurate.

The man told him the trip would be rough at first, but after a few minutes, as they cleared the worst of the storms, things would settle. They had nothing to do but wait until someone opened the doors from the outside.

Luke Umble could barely see his wife's face in the dimly lit room. He tried to remember the last time he saw her smile. Things had been bad over the past weeks and months. He could only think of Annie with that strained look on her face. He hoped she would smile when they opened the doors. However, even he had no idea what to expect. The only thing Luke knew for sure was that their old life was over. Salvation waited on the other side of those doors and when they opened, their new life would start.

Two

Discovery

The grinding of metal and a sudden jolting stop to their movement brought everyone to silence. The transport reached its destination.

Luke Umble held his breath. In his thoughts and prayers, he knew he made the right choice. He knew he saved his family. Until the good Lord cradled them all, they would never truly be saved. This was their best option on Earth. Now, Luke wondered if their physical salvation would be worse than sacrificing their lives. For centuries, the Amish walked apart from the *Englische*. It seemed the *Englische* ruined the planet, yet they offered the only solution to continue living. Once those heavy metal doors opened, Luke could decide if following the *Englische* was the best choice.

He put his hand on his wife's shoulder and she flinched. She must not have expected his touch in the dim room, crowded with strangers. He loved her for her unquestioning support, but their relationship had become strained. Everyone's had over the past few months as their world seemed to fall apart around them. The weather conditions gradually worsened and human relations seemed to mirror that. The curve of Annie's shoulder felt strange to Luke. It had been some time since he last touched her in a loving way. His reassurance came from the fact that she did not pull away from him. They still had love in their marriage, but it was being tested.

All things were being tested.

After the moment of silence, the doors hissed. Hidden mechanical controls forced the rubber seals apart and the doors slowly opened. Luke knew they would be carried on the small transport for only a short time. He knew they would switch to a larger transport and there would be someone to give them instructions. Other than that, he had no idea what waited on the other side of those exceptionally slow doors.

As soon as they opened wide enough, a young *Neufremdefreund* squeezed through. His impatient action caused a stir and instantly everyone started pushing toward the opening. It appeared that no one wanted to wait for the doors. Luke saw people shoving past Katie's wheelchair. Her brother John did his best to keep the panicky people from knocking the little girl out of it. Luke admired his son and daughter for keeping their calm. Katie waited in her chair and John did not try to force the stubborn contraption out. As such, the Umble family stepped out of the transport last.

Luke watched friends and strangers clear the opening and move into a long room with a low ceiling. Most of them made it about ten steps, some farther, but once they looked to their left, every one of them stopped. Many dropped to their knees. Luke could not see what caught their attention, but he had his suspicions. He had been anticipating this moment.

Mostly, he cared to see the reactions of his family. None of them knew where they were going.

Katie's wheelchair rolled smoothly over the brown metal floor. The narrow slits in the floor allowed filtered air through, but did not impede the old chair. Luke helped John lift Katie over the threshold between the transport and the long room. *Englische* dressed in baby-blue coveralls directed everyone to keep moving forward. They tried to get people clear of the transports so that the doors could automatically close.

Luke looked to his right to see three other transports unloading. It reminded him of one of the larger dairy farms where hundreds of cattle herded through a series of wide barn doors. At the far end of the room, which was filling fast, he could see four other transport doors. One remained closed; two looked as crowded as the one he stepped from a moment ago. The third held less than a dozen people. It seemed not everyone made it to their departure times. This long, low room served as a hub for eight transports. The people that came from those transports all shared similar expressions of fear and confusion. Only the baby-blue *Englische* seemed to know what was happening, but not even all of them looked confident.

"Oh papa!" exclaimed Katie.

Luke turned to his daughter. Katie and the family looked to the left with the rest of the crowd. His wife gasped. Like so many others, she dropped to her knees in prayer, clenching baby Matthew to her bosom.

"What have you done, my son?" said Levi Umble from Luke's shoulder. Disappointment dripped from his words, causing Luke to break his gaze at the new sight and turn to his father for an instant. The old man looked angry beyond words, but Luke did not have time for that now. Luke had disappointed his father before and he would likely do it again. Never intentional, it was the nature of their relationship. Right now, Luke wanted to see what all of the others had already seen. He needed to see it to help him confirm he made the right choice.

Luke moved away from his father and wife. He stepped past his other four children to get an unobstructed view. The long, left wall appeared to be mostly windows. Luke guessed they were divided into twelve foot sections with that brown metal separating them and holding them in place. Everything seemed to be made of that brown metal, dull and dark. Pale yellow lights glowed from each post that segmented the windows. The depressing atmosphere would take some getting used to, Luke acknowledged.

Inspecting or admiring the construction of their new home would have to wait. All that mattered now was what he saw on the other side of that thick glass. He knew it had to be thick. Considering that it stood between them and certain death, it probably was not even glass, but some kind of *Englische* devised synthetic.

Luke stepped up to the window. His heart beat faster and his breath felt thick, clogging his throat. He exhaled with effort and fogged the glass. Luke had to wipe it away with a trembling hand. He blinked at a sight that he never dreamed he would see. The Earth did not look like it had in his old school books. Instead of being a glorious blue marble, it mostly looked brown and dying. Gray clouds covered parts of the planet. Luke could see lightning snapping through the massive cyclones, like the one that tore apart his father's home. He could make out the Northwest United States and an erupting volcano. The explosive force of the mountain exuded so much orange lava that it could be seen from this distance.

None of it seemed real, but Luke knew they were in space.

Some people prayed. Others wailed. Luke stood in awe. The *Englische* said the Earth would not sustain life for much longer. He had his doubts, but relied on his own prayers to decide to accompany the *Englische* in the search for a new planet.

Luke looked around the hazy planet and saw more transports presumably carrying others. He did not know whether to think of them as survivors, refugees or escapees. The transports flew to other ships close by. The size of these transports left him agape. He had built a few barns in his time and even worked some construction. His mind could barely grasp the scope of these massive ships and the resources to construct them.

A few of the rectangular pods came toward the ship on which he now stood. They disappeared below his line of sight, which told him this behemoth had more than one level. Studying one of the neighboring vessels, he saw that they had at least ten levels with pods docking on almost all of them. One of the transport pods did not seem to slow as it neared. Luke worried that it was going to collide with them. Uncomfortably close, the pod changed directions, veering back toward Earth. It angled into the path of another pod and the two disintegrated before his eyes.

Luke could not even blink. He had no idea how many people were on those pods. All that remained were spiraling fragments of metal hanging at the cusp of the Earth's gravity. He involuntarily prayed for the safe delivery of their souls. With the enormous ships, the crash and the dying planet, Luke could not avert his eyes.

It took a tug on his pant leg from his son to bring him back to reality.

"Are we in space, Pa?" asked Henry.

"That we are, my son," said Luke. He tried to hide the waver in his voice. Looking back at the planet, Luke felt sorrow for what the human race had done to God's beautiful creation. So much careless action, so much the quest for greed. He wondered if the Amish could not have been a better example. Maybe they could have shown the world a better way. Luke Umble promised himself if they were starting over that he would stand in front of all men and show them the Lord's way.

Henry interrupted Luke's thoughts again. He said, "What about the animals?"

"What animals?" asked Luke.

Henry's face turned to a frown. He looked upset at not having a clear response. He said, "Any of them. I see lots of people, but no animals. Noah's Ark is supposed to have animals."

A young *Englische* woman heard Henry's question. She bent over to answer him and her blue coveralls folded counter to the recently pressed creases. She said, "Well, this isn't Noah's Ark, it's called the Corinthian. It is one of sixteen vessels commissioned by Adam Corp. The good news is we do have animals. Would you like to see them?"

Henry looked to his father and Luke nodded. Even in this strange situation, it made Luke feel good that his children remembered their manners and showed him respect. The *Englische* woman must have seen Luke's approval. She pulled a small pad from one of her many pockets and pressed it with her finger. Light from the screen illuminated her face.

"I'll arrange a tour for you then. Now hold still," she said. The *Englische* held her pad up vertically and a light flashed across Henry's face. She turned the pad around to show Henry that she took his picture. The image showed the boy with his eyes squeezed shut. The *Englische* woman continued, "Umble family, would you please join our group here? I am Crewman P1114. This vessel has twelve levels. We are currently on Level Six and I am taking you to your assigned living quarters down on Level Eight. Please stay close and listen for your name."

P1114 led them to the wall opposite the windows. Luke looked to the now sealed transport doors on either side of them while they stood as the herd of people waited for their turn on the small elevators that seemed to buzz with excitement. Some of his fear subsided once he moved away from the windows. He watched Katie repeatedly turn her chair to take another look at the Earth. Each time, John promptly turned her back toward the elevators.

The *Englische* woman looked down at Henry as he fidgeted. "You can call me Mindi," she said.

Eventually, their turn for the elevator came. Somehow, they managed to cram four families into the little space. It seemed the ship kept getting smaller and smaller as they progressed. When the elevator doors opened, they stepped into a long, narrow hall. Luke could easily touch both side walls without fully extending his arms. He knew Annie would not like this much. She did not care for small spaces. He wanted to reach out and comfort his wife, but three people stood between them. Lately, it felt like there was always something in between them.

As Mindi, aka P1114, led them down the hall, she pressed buttons on her computer pad. Occasionally, a door would open and she would call out a family name. Down the length of the hall, their party shrank as families disappeared into their new living quarters. The entire time, Henry did not stop asking questions.

"Mindi, how many animals are there? What are the names of the other ships? Why can't we stay on Level Six? Do you have any puppies? When can we go to Level One? Why do the numbers go down instead of up? Does this spaceship have electricity? We don't use electricity. Is it always nighttime in space? What other animals are on the ship? Where do we get food? Where do we go to the bathroom?"

In polite conversation, Luke would have stopped his son's incessant questioning with a stern look. This time, he let him go because he, too, wanted to hear the answers to some of those questions. Sadly, Mindi managed to avoid the answers. Her only reply was, "I can tell you more when we take the tour. Umble family, these are your new quarters."

A plain, brown metal door whisked open and yellow light spilled out into the hall. Mindi did not wait for any of them to enter before she headed back down the length of corridor toward the elevator. John wheeled Katie through the door first. Luke waved a hand to usher the rest of his family inside, but Annie hesitated. She put her head down next to Matthew's as she cradled him. The baby seemed to be taking it well, no crying the entire time.

Levi led Henry and Mary into their quarters. Luke stood in the hall with his wife. He said, "Come, let us enter our new home together."

Annie looked at him as if he slapped her across the face. He could never recall a look like that from her. She said, "Home? Our home is on solid ground and provided for by the Lord's bounty. This is no home. This is cold and cramped. This is an *Englische* contrivance designed to carry us away from God."

"Did you not look out that window?" asked Luke. "There is no home back there. There is no life. I think even God gave up on that planet."

Annie stared hard at him. He knew what she was thinking. He had never in his life blasphemed. Luke hurriedly revised his position.

"I know that our Father, the creator of Heaven and Earth, is with us in our hearts always. Wherever this vessel carries us, we will carry His glory," Luke said.

His wife dropped her eyes, snuggled Matthew and walked silently into their quarters. Luke followed her into the low-ceilinged, square room. He could not believe that was their new living space, one big room. Then he noticed doors on the surrounding walls. No hinges, no knobs. Only solid brown plates that meshed with the walls. Three doors on the left wall, two in front and two to the right. Discovering what waited behind those doors would come later. His family demanded his attention.

John positioned Katie at the end of a bench that tried to pass itself off as a couch. He and Mary sat on the uncomfortable-looking metallic couch. Across from them, Henry bounced his knees on the cushion of a chair. Annie settled with Matthew on another matching chair. Levi stood with his arms folded. Luke studied the faces of people he thought he knew so well. At this moment, he felt like he was in a room full of strangers.

Luke could read John, Mary and Henry the easiest. They all seemed excited. Their wide eyes and uncontrollable grins reassured him. Along with youth came curiosity. Three of his children would have enjoyed this opportunity under any circumstances. Luke turned from Henry's bright face to Annie's. He already knew what his wife thought. Only time would allow them to come together again. That left two members of his family, his father and his disease-stricken daughter. So many times in his life, the thoughts and feelings of these two swayed him more than any other.

Katie's wheelchair kept her from exploring her world, but somehow her insight reached farther than the most widely travelled. The look on her face showed Luke hope, but sadness. He would ask her about it, but not in front of the others. Her look almost made him doubt his choice of bringing them here.

Levi, however, left no question as to his opinion. With a scowl, he said, "You have destroyed this family. You have abandoned your faith. You stood in my house and lied to me."

"I never lied." Luke tried to defend his position.

"You said you were taking us someplace safe," countered Levi. "Casting us into the void in a tin box full of *Englische* is nowhere safe that I know of."

Luke said, "Maybe we should not discuss this in front of the *kinder*."

"Why not? It would be the first honest thing they heard from their father," snapped Levi.

The words hit Luke hard and seemed to suck the air out of his chest. Since his mother died, his relationship with Levi had been a challenge. They exchanged heated words on many subjects over the years, but always ended in reconciliation. This time, it seemed Levi lashed out from a place of anger. Accusations of lying and abandoning his faith hurt Luke far worse than his father's old hickory switch from his boyhood scoldings.

"I did not lie," Luke repeated.

He faltered. He wanted to stand up to his father, but he did not know if that was the right thing to show his own children. No one else spoke. Luke felt like he was on a stage and the audience hung on his every word and action. Finally, he said, "I saved our faith. There was nothing back there for us, for the human race. My decision, and mine alone, saved this family."

"Oh, so you are our savior? Those are prideful words," said Levi.

"Do not speak to me of pride," said Luke. He felt himself losing his temper. Doing such would be one of the worst things he could do in front of his children. Arguing with his father already showed too much disrespect for everyone in the room. Luke tried to control himself and lowered his voice. "This family has already sacrificed much. I could not bear to see us lose anything else. I did not lie to anyone, but I admit I did not tell the whole truth. If I had, half of us would not be here right now. I said I would take us someplace safe and I have. This *Englische* vessel will carry us to a new world where we can start over. For that, I think we should thank God."

Before Luke could start a prayer, Levi said, "Do you know anything of these *Englische*? Who is this

Adam Corporation? I worry that they have tricked you and you, in turn, tricked us. That is the way of the *Englische*. Deceit comes easy to them. If you choose to follow their path, you already know where it leads. This time, you have brought your whole family with you."

"Let us pray," said Luke. He had no other response for his father now. Silence would be better than arguing. He bowed his head and one by one, his family followed. In the midst of their silent prayer, something started beeping. Everyone started looking around to see what made such a sound. Henry pointed at the front door of their quarters. Luke saw the flashing red light that caught his son's attention.

Henry said, "I think someone is at the door."

As Luke approached the door to the hall, it opened on its own, sliding into the wall. Crewman P1114 stood in the entryway, a glistening smile showed her extremely straight, extremely white teeth.

"Greetings, Umble family," said Mindi. "I hope you have found your quarters acceptable."

"Uh," started Luke. He wanted to ask about beds and other necessities.

"Where's the bathroom?" interrupted Henry. Luke heard Levi snicker somewhere behind him.

"May I come in?" asked Mindi.

Luke gestured an invitation with his right hand. Mindi walked into the room and navigated it in a clockwise pattern. As she neared the first door on her left, it slid open without even touching a button. Mindi walked into the room and the family rose from their seats to watch her. After a moment, a large section of the wall slid down to reveal a pass-through window.

"This is the kitchen," she said.

Looking in the window, Luke could see a short counter where he imagined the *kinder* could eat breakfast. If they had stools, they would sit in the main room and Annie could easily hand the food to them. As sure as he thought it, four seats automatically extended out of the wall on his side of the counter. They actually could sit there. The kitchen looked small and appeared to have more gadgets than his wife would ever use or want.

"What do you expect me to do in here?" asked Annie. She shifted Matthew to her left hip as she leaned through the kitchen door.

"The kitchen is intended for food preparation," said Mindi. The answer would have sounded sarcastic coming from anyone else, but the crewman's expression did not reflect a flippant attitude.

"Give me a pot, a pan, a sharp knife and a good spatula. I don't push buttons when I cook," countered Annie.

Mindi looked slightly confused. "You have every convenience at your disposal. Is it not to your liking?"

Annie walked out of the kitchen. She mumbled, "It's not supposed to be convenient. It's supposed to be the way my mother taught me and her mother taught her before that. Convenience is for the lazy. I work to feed my family."

Luke heard only part of what Annie grumbled. The look he caught from her said the rest. He knew his wife felt similar to his father about their new situation. She respected him enough not to say too much in front of the rest of the family.

Mindi left the kitchen and opened the second door. She said, "This is your laundry washing facility."

"I wash everything by hand," said Annie. "I won't need those machines."

Mindi stared at Annie for a moment. She opened her mouth as if to speak and abruptly closed it. The almost unnatural smile disappeared for a moment and Mindi's eyes seemed to gloss. Then the smile returned and Mindi went back to normal. "No worries," she said.

Apparently without any other concerns, Mindi opened the third door on the left wall. She said, "This is your Physical Waste Disposal facility."

"Our what?" asked John.

Henry ran into the small, closet-like room and stretched a hose from the wall. He cheerfully exclaimed, "The bathroom."

"If required, I can demonstrate the proper use of the facility," offered Mindi.

Luke said, "I don't think that will be necessary." He felt himself blushing on behalf of the entire family. At the last moment, he stopped Henry from putting the funnel end of the hose on his face. Luke heard the hose make a sucking sound as he guided it back into the wall socket.

Mindi seemed to be in full tour guide mode. She did not wait for any of them to finish investigating the bathroom. She moved along the next wall and opened both of the doors. John pushed Katie into one of the rooms and Mary and Henry checked out the other one.

"These are the juvenile bedrooms," said Mindi. While the kinder went back and forth between the rooms, Mindi led the way to the final two doors of their new quarters. She said, "This is the primary bedroom and the other is the auxiliary room."

Luke thought the primary bedroom looked almost as big as the two juvenile rooms combined. However, the auxiliary room seemed almost as small as the bathroom.

"What is this auxiliary room?" huffed Levi.

"I think it is your bedroom, *Daed*," said Luke with a grin. It may not have been ideal, but Luke was glad his father would not have to share a room with the boys. All in all, with the revelation of the additional rooms and facilities, Luke felt better than when he first walked in to the square chamber. It bothered him a little that they did not have any windows. He would miss watching the sunrise.

Back in the center of the main room, Mindi demonstrated to Annie how to lower the dining table from the ceiling. Mary took her baby brother from Annie. Luke watched his wife absorb the new information. He knew she would be resistant to the electronic devices, but she studied the *Englische* crewman in order to perform her familial duties.

Out of the corner of his eye, Luke watched his father carry his tattered suitcase into the auxiliary room. None of them had any choice but to make the best of their situation. He suspected Levi would not complain much in front of the kinder. It would take some adapting, but Luke felt more and more comfortable in his decision.

"Is the Umble family ready to continue the tour?" asked Mindi.

Luke took hold of the handles on Katie's chair. He wanted to be close to her and see her reactions to the rest of the ship. He said, "*Ja*, please lead the way."

Mindi led the family back along the narrow hallway. Luke could feel the strobe of Katie's wheels riding along the perforated floor. He knew it could not feel good for her, but she was always strong. At their last doctor's visit, he prescribed some painkillers in addition to her normal medicines. She had yet to take one. Luke prayed that he might share a fraction of her strength.

As the elevator doors opened, Mindi said, "The Corinthian has twelve levels. Level One is Administration and Navigation and Level Twelve is Engineering. Ten levels are reserved for food production. Animals are housed on the outer decks, while crops are centralized. The majority of living quarters are found at the fore and aft of the Corinthian. The crops are organized by total water consumption, rice and grains on the upper decks, vegetables and fruits in the mid-decks and citrus and tropical on the sub-decks. The Corinthian has a completely self-contained water system, but we will discuss that more later."

Luke felt like he understood maybe half of what Mindi said. It astounded him that they could grow anything on board a space ship. He had been away from his crops so long that he wished to see anything green and growing. The dry Earth had not yield a single sprout and he missed that natural connection to his Maker.

"We will pass through Level Three to see the assigned crop of Luke and John Umble. You should be familiar with wheat and oats," continued Mindi as the elevator carried them upward. Luke knew there would be work to do on board. He had not had much discussion with the *Englische* in that regard. It felt strange that he and his oldest son would be assigned a specific area, but he would do what needed to be done.

Henry danced like he needed to go to the bathroom. He said, "If this ship is called the Corinthian, what are the other ships called?"

Mindi turned and smiled at Henry as she had done when they first met. She explained, "Adam Corp was commissioned by a coalition of Earth governments to construct a fleet of space faring vehicles. Due to time restraints and budget limitations, only sixteen ships were completed. They are identified as follows: Genesis, Exodus, Leviticus, Nehemiah, Ecclesiastes, Lamentation, Obadiah, Jonah, Corinthian, Galatian, Philippian, Colossian, Thessalonian, Titus, Philemon and Revelation."

"But those are all books of the Bible," chimed Mary.

"Correct," said Mindi. "The executive board of Adam Corp issued a statement regarding the naming of the vessels as symbolic pertaining to the primarily Judeo-Christian contingency."

The elevator seemed to be taking a while. It moved slowly and gave Luke plenty of time to process the new information. He said, "Are you saying that only Christians and Jews were allowed to leave Earth?"

Mindi's smile disappeared again. It was almost like her consciousness went with it. Then she came back to attention. She said, "Not at all. Two of our vessels carry non-Judeo-Christians exclusively. The Corinthian is the only vessel to carry those of the Christian denomination known as Amish."

The elevator doors whooshed open, ending that conversation. After a few twists and turns, the tour group emerged into a massive room. Blazing lights overhead confused Luke's senses. He almost felt like he was out in the middle of his field. A slight breeze drifted from a huge circular vent on the nearby wall. In front of them, rows of new wheat poked out of fresh black soil.

Luke wanted to say how beautiful it looked, but Mindi spoke before him. She said, "Each level contains approximately one point four-four million square feet of producible land. That is roughly equivalent to twenty-five fields of the previously banned sport known as American Football."

John stepped up. Luke thought he looked equally as excited. "Did you say one million square feet?" John asked.

"One million, four hundred, forty-thousand to be more exact," corrected Mindi. "You will find the same amount of usable area on each of the ten food production levels. It has been determined as adequate to feed the ten thousand passenger allowance of each vessel."

The size of the vessel already impressed Luke. He did not truly realize the scope of the endeavor until now. In many ways, their life was completely different, but in many others, it seemed that it would stay the same. Obviously, they had to eat on their journey. It had not occurred to him where they would get the food. The concept of a self-contained vehicle seemed divinely inspired.

Mindi did not allow them to linger long. While she appeared to have a pleasant disposition, she was all business. Luke wondered what about the *Englische* caused her to be so exact and formal. Those kinds of questions were not for a married man to ask a young lady. He conceded that her personal life was her own and let the thoughts stray from his head.

Next they visited Level One and the Bridge. Mindi introduced them to the *Englische* captain. She said, "Umble family, this is Captain Sam Nixon."

Captain Nixon finished saying his goodbyes to another tour group. Luke did not recognize that Amish family. The captain joined them with a broad grin. He looked like the sort that enjoyed meeting new people, or at least, putting on a display for them. His command area was defined by a series of rails that formed a square around his large, comfortable-looking chair and a sprawling desk. Behind him, rows of what looked like office desks filled the room. People, busy on computers, did not look up from their work.

"Welcome aboard the Corinthian. You can call me Captain Sam," he said. His smile looked permanently fixed over his protruding chin. The man had dark eyes and a muscular build. Luke suspected he was chosen to be captain for his physical appearance as much as any skill he might possess. The broad shouldered man stood several inches taller than Luke. He looked like he could be intimidating if need be. Those under his command would likely follow his orders due to his natural charisma or threat of bodily harm.

"Captain Sam?" asked Henry.

"Yes, young...what do you people say? *Kinner*?" replied the captain.

"Some do, but our church says *kinder*," said Annie. Luke appreciated that his wife spoke her mind in most any situation.

A momentary look of annoyance bounced off the captain's face and vanished. "Well, *kinder*, what can I do for you?"

"My name's Henry and I want to know where you are taking us."

The captain stood to his full height. He got a faraway look in his eyes and turned toward the wide window at the other end of the Bridge. He said, "That is an excellent question. The real answer, I have left up to the best scientists and astronomers at Adam Corp. My job is to follow their instructions. But you see that star there?" Captain Sam pointed toward the window at no particular star. "That is where I'm taking you."

Luke thought he sounded half sincere, but got the uneasy feeling that the captain of this incredible ship had no real idea where they were going.

Captain Sam added, "P1114 can explain it much better than I can." Then the captain turned his back and sat in his command chair. Luke got another feeling that the man was not entirely sincere. He was *Englische* and some of them had prejudice toward the Amish, especially after the mass conversions over the last decade.

P1114, or Mindi, tugged at the front of her coveralls to straighten them. The light blue material matched her twinkling eyes. She said, "The purpose of the Adam Corp fleet is to follow an extrasolar trajectory to reach a spectral class G or K star, ideally a red dwarf. Star JER-29.11 seems to be within acceptable parameters. Several of these stars in this class have been identified as having Earth-like planets in life sustaining orbits."

Luke pondered how much the *Englische* could possibly know about other planets orbiting their sun or some other star. Their government-run space agencies only went to the moon a few times. Luke only knew of one private company that completed a manned mission to Mars. Despite all of their technology and idealism, he suspected they actually knew very little of the universe. He felt like his father in thinking if God wanted us to fly, he would have given us wings. In this case, God did not give them space suits either.

The *Englische* made a compelling argument when Luke first considered bringing his family on board. No one he knew wanted to remain behind on a dying planet. The *Englische* promised a new, unspoiled world where Amish ways would be revered and respected. The *Englische* openly admitted the mistakes they made on Earth in their drive for new technology and machinations. They said that same mistake would not be allowed on their new planet. Luke wanted to save his family and had thoughts of saving the human race by leading as an example. It seemed the *Englische* exodus was the only option, but now he wondered how much they really knew about their destination. Luke left the bridge feeling unsure of Captain Sam and his crew.

Everywhere they went on their tour, those dull brown walls seemed to press in on them. Once they made it to the engine room, it only seemed more claustrophobic. In parts, they had to walk with ducked heads and Mindi continuously reminded them not to touch the thick pipes on either side. Steam escaped some of the couplings and Luke surmised the water inside must be incredibly hot.

As they walked, Mindi explained, "Adam Corp is a people company. We do not restrict access to any area of the ship. It is requested that if you have not been trained in a particular facility that you remain clear of that area." She spoke as if she had given this tour hundreds of times. It sounded memorized and lacked emotion. She gestured to the walls, "The black pipes that you see are carrying super-heated water from our main reactor."

John seemed to take more interest as they neared the engine room. Something about the inner workings of the ship must have appealed to him, Luke suspected. He walked close to Mindi and asked, "Does that mean this vessel is nuclear powered?"

Mindi did not answer at first. She led the family around another corner in this labyrinth on the lowest level of the Corinthian. Luke started noticing white pipes running alongside the black ones. On the white pipes, he saw little labels that read *Clean* or *Potable* or *Do Not Exceed 45 Degrees Fahrenheit*. Apparently, white was good and black was bad. He assumed water was a major component of the ship's engine.

Stepping through a hatchway that would have been equally at home on a submarine, Mindi pointed at a glass wall in a room that could have spanned the four lowest decks of the ship. Metal ladders and platforms spread around the tank like a skeletal scaffold. Mindi said, "This storage tank holds three million gallons of water. It is routed through two systems. The open system provides for all of the agricultural needs and human consumption. The closed system provides the coolant for the nuclear reactor."

"It is nuclear," spouted John.

Mindi put her hand on John's shoulder. The gesture looked awkward to Luke, as if she had not done something like that before. She said, "The reactor powers internal operations, filtration, air control…"

"It also powers my baby," said a female voice.

The Umble family turned to see a young woman climbing down the scaffolding along the side of the water tank. The curly blond woman did not offer much in stature, but she made up for it in attitude and spirit. Luke could immediately tell she loved her work and was used to being in control of her environment. The other thing he could tell was how John responded to her. He straightened his shoulders and took a step away from Mindi. Despite her sweaty face and dirty hands, she did not look much older than John and even Luke thought she was cute.

"This is Chief Engineer…" started Mindi.

The young woman interrupted their guide for a second time. She said, "Call me Huxtable. My team calls me Hux. The nuclear reactor's primary job is to power the VASIMR engine. It's what gives Cori her thrust."

"Who is Cori?" asked Luke.

"The ship, Pa. Cori is obviously short for Corinthian," nudged John.

Mary stepped up next to her brother. Luke had seen pretty girls vie for John's attention before. He knew Mary was not doing that, but she probably was a little jealous, a typical trait of teenage girls. At sixteen, Mary was every bit as attractive as this Huxtable. In her time, Luke knew his daughter would have no problem finding a good man.

Mary asked, "What is a Vasi…engine?"

"VASIMR," stated Huxtable. "It means Variable Specific Impulse Magnetoplasma Rocket. In other words, it is a giant electro-magnet that heats ions for thrust. At maximum velocity, I'm anticipating travel at one tenth the speed of light."

Luke could barely process the information. This whole tour made him feel like they walked into a make-believe world. If he felt lost, he wondered how Annie was feeling.

His father, however, made his feelings known. Levi waved both of his hands at Huxtable. "You are speaking a foreign language. I have had enough of this so-called tour."

"Can we see it?" asked John. He moved closer to Huxtable. She looked up into his face and they seemed to be sharing a private moment.

Mindi said, "No one outside of the Engineering team is allowed into the VASIMR chamber."

Luke recalled that Mindi said that they do not restrict access to any area. Now, she is telling a different story. He wanted to question her, but John beat him to it.

"Why can't we have a look?"

Huxtable answered for Mindi which earned a sideways glance from the tour guide. Luke got the feeling that these two *Englische* did not usually get along. The engineer said, "It is not forbidden, but unadvised. We like to keep as many people away from the *Vas* while she is heating up. It takes time for the engine to come to full power. Our departure from Earth will be the first full-speed test. I don't want to take any unnecessary risks."

Every answer spawned two or three new questions. Huxtable did not seem worried about the engine, but it bothered Luke that they would be having their *first* full-speed test only now that all of their passengers were on board. Luke would like very much to have a sit-down conversation with the captain, but it would have to wait. At some point, he would have to get answers. He felt entitled to at least that.

Mindi led the family from the Engine Room back to their quarters. They passed several other tour groups. Luke recognized one of the families and thanked God that they made it aboard.

After Mindi bade them a good night, everyone seemed to relax a little. Levi went toward his bedroom. The door did not open immediately and he bumped into it. He already seemed agitated by the discussion of *Englische* technology. Having it misfire on him would not help his mood.

Mindi may have said good night, but Luke had no way to know for certain what time it was. Even on the bridge, he saw no sun to give him reference. It had been mid-day when they left their farm, but it could have been hours since then. Luke found a digital clock in the kitchen that told him it was one fourteen. That must be in the morning, he surmised. Their adrenalin kept them going for hours past their normal bedtime.

Returning to the main room, Luke found Henry asleep on the strange couch. The boy mumbled in his sleep, "We didn't get to see the animals."

Annie had already retired to their bedroom with baby Matthew. Mary and Katie choose the bedroom on the left. Luke decided to leave Henry where he lay.

"Pa?" asked John. "Can we talk?"

Luke stroked his beard. His mind wandered as he imagined what John would look like with a beard. "We should talk in the morning. Now is time for sleep. When we wake, I will find us clean clothes and we will prepare for work on Level Three."

John started to turn toward his new bedroom and stopped. He said, "That is what I wanted to talk to you about. I would like to work in the Engineering Room."

Luke weighed his son's words. He felt sure they were influenced by a pretty smile and gentle curves.

He countered, "The Umbles have always worked the land. What do you know of technical things?"

"I know something of the mechanical and I've always been a fast learner," said John.

"That you have," said Luke. He put his hand on his son's shoulder. It was no longer the soft shoulder of a boy, but the muscular rock of a man. Luke would not stand in the way of a man making his own decisions, but he wanted John to make it for the right reasons.

"In the morning, we will talk with your mother. She will remind you of your obligations to the faith, but you have yet to be baptized," finished Luke.

"*Danki*," said John. He hugged his father, something he had not done in a while. Luke liked the feeling, but it was strange. He had not hugged his own father in a long time. He was used to the soft embrace of his daughters.

"*Ja*, in the morning," repeated Luke

.

Three

Peregrination

It felt like a dream.

Luke could feel that familiar trickle of sweat running down the back of his neck. When he bent over, his shirt pressed cool against the sweat in the small of his back. They had perfect growing weather. The combination of bright sunlight and a soft breeze put the temperature at about eighty degrees. Luke could tell that without looking at a thermometer. He spent enough time outdoors in his life that years ago he stopped looking at his mother's old thermometer hanging by the kitchen door. He liked the faded red rooster sitting on top of the cheap plastic, but it had no other value for him than nostalgia.

Luke dug his fingers into the damp soil. He could feel the small pebbles and watched the deep brown and rich black earth fall to the ground. He thought about how perfect the mix was. It really did seem like a dream.

Already, the new crop stood about knee high. Rows of bright green plants surrounded him. It would not be long before the wheat grew to waist height and turned that heart-warming golden color. The dream would have been that much sweeter with John at his side. But his oldest son chose a different path in their new life.

Luke plucked the straw hat from his head. He wiped his forehead with a handkerchief that his oldest daughter had embroidered his name on almost ten years ago. One of the corners was mostly frayed and the thing had long ago given up trying to be white. Yellow and brown stains that would never wash out represented to him a lifetime of hard, honest work. As he dabbed the beads of sweat on his forehead, he thought about the other men who worked the field with him. After only a few days travel from Earth, they stopped wearing their hats. They reasoned that they were always indoors now. Luke did not feel the same. He wanted to maintain the custom and keep his humility. That is why he kept this hat on when working the fields. He could feel the warmth of the sun on his scalp and did not want a sun burn. Luke hoped for a moment's respite from its heat, but the artificial sun never set on Level Three.

That constant reminder stole Luke out of his dream and locked him back in his reality. In this reality, Luke did not keep track of a normal work day. He stayed in the fields until he felt the need for food or rest. He knew they had a long journey ahead of them and decided to pass most of the time with work. He found many of his Amish brethren to be of similar mind. He felt an obligation and duty to the work. Despite a few passing conversations with his wife, Luke put the needs of the ship before the needs of his family.

Certain parts of the day, the lights dimmed, but it never got truly dark. Luke knew the plants needed more dark, but the *Englische* had other ideas. One of the crewmen in a blue jumpsuit told a computer when the sun should set. It gave Luke pause to consider one man had that much power. The *Englische* seemed always to be challenging God. Not only were they in search of a new Eden, but they could control the sun and rain en route. Luke had yet to find the opportunity to question their scheduling methods. He knew the plants needed more dark and hoped they would last under these bright conditions until he could address the *Englische*. No clouds ever darkened this field either. Rain came from overhead sprinklers as the water trickled down from Level Two. It seemed very sensible not to waste the water. At least he understood a few of their ideas. The plants got what they needed and the rest ran off in long drains at the end of each row. He knew it sank down to the next level, but Luke had yet to venture to Level Four. He could not say for sure what they grew there. It did not matter to him; his work was here.

Barely separating night and day in his head and working the new field for countless hours made it all seem like a dream.

It was a good dream.

It also felt good to have a new hat after losing his in the storm. One of their new neighbors had a knack for weaving. The older lady wanted to contribute and in less than two days had a small pile of straw hats ready. Luke let his new hat plop back on his head. It rested with a slight tilt backwards; he did not need the brim to block any glare from the sun. He stretched with his hands pressed into his lower back on either side. Those muscles seemed to speak to him, saying, "You have done good. We are worn out. Now leave us be."

"Ack," said Luke. "My back did not complain so much twenty years ago, or even five. Father, give me strength to do Your bidding. If I am sore at forty, what will I be at sixty? My spirit is strong and I need a body to match."

The soft breeze answered him. High up on the far wall, large fan blades spun aimlessly. They circulated the air enough to bring peace and silence to Luke Umble. Luke focused on the peace. He assumed that is how his God would respond to him and not simply with silence.

Looking out across the field, Luke spied a boy running toward him. It could have been his son, Henry, but like too many of the other Amish, this boy did not wear his hat. The small figure grew more recognizable as he neared. Luke could tell for certain that it was Henry. Luke felt like his family should be setting an example. Maybe Henry was having fun, but he would put a stop to that and discipline the boy on the spot.

Then it occurred to Luke that Henry was not running like a boy at play. He ran with a purpose, like there was some kind of emergency.

"Pa," Henry shouted, still a good hundred feet away from his father. "Come quick. He did it again!"

Henry did not have to say anything more. Luke knew who *he* was and what he *did* again. Luke's father Levi had been the most resistant to leaving their home. He continued to be the most resistant to their new circumstances. Luke expected this. However, he did not expect Levi to continually lock himself in his room.

As Luke ran back to their quarters with Henry, he recounted the argument of the previous days. Winding through the narrow, brown corridors, Luke thought his father made sense, in a way. The doors operated on sensors controlled by computers. Levi maintained that he would have nothing to do with electricity. He refused to use the fluorescent lights in his room, but they were automatic and motion sensitive, unless the inhabitant used the computer to indicate he or she was going to sleep. Levi had Henry turn off the lights and then he tried to burn a candle. The automatic fire suppression system put a stop to that immediately. So for Levi Umble, the lights stayed on and the door stayed closed.

With each passing day, Levi escalated in his determination to avoid the computers. Only the day before, he somehow managed to stick the door closed. He insisted if it did not have a handle that he could use, then he would not use the door at all. Luke knew his father must have wedged it closed again.

Annie greeted Luke at the door to their quarters. His wife's disapproving look silently told him that his father's behavior was partly his responsibility. In one of their late night conversations, she used the word *fault*. Annie made her feelings known and mostly she felt confused. Their conversations never came to full blown arguments, but they came close. He understood that she felt misled and lost, but he could not make her completely understand that his actions were for the salvation of the whole family.

Inside, Henry jumped up on the couch to watch the two *Englische* already prying at the door. Luke wondered for a passing moment why they were here, but then took action to open his father's door. He looked for John to assist, but John was not there. He spent his time as an engineer's apprentice and was gone as much as Luke. The thought of John's absence could send Luke down a different path. He ignored those thoughts and concentrated on the door.

The *Englische* stepped aside. The evidently older of the two said, "We received an alert that the controls had been damaged. My apologies for the intrusion, but we are required to see to the safety of everyone on board, even in their personal quarters."

Luke nodded his understanding. He pressed his ear against the unfriendly, cold metal and said, "*Daed*, can you hear me?"

No response.

Too many thoughts went through Luke's head. What if his father tried to light another candle? He could be suffocating or drowning or whatever happens in a sealed room in space. They had not had the best relationship in recent years, but Luke dreaded the idea of losing his father, especially right after he saved him.

"Levi Umble, open this door!"

"I cannot," said Levi, his voice faint through the door.

Luke breathed a sigh of relief. At least the old man was alive. Luke asked, "Why can you not open it?"

"I've smashed the controls," came the reply. He had gone too far this time. Luke felt it was one thing for his father to lock himself in the room. It was not acceptable to damage someone else's property. After all, the Corinthian did not belong to them.

Luke turned to the *Englische*. The younger of the two held a tool that looked like a motorized pry bar. Luke nodded and the young man went to work. He seemed to have a non-verbal understanding with these *Englische*. Maybe, he thought, they recognized him as a leader among his people.

In a matter of moments, the young *Englische* pried open the door. He must have broken something in the process. A purple liquid sprayed out of the crack at the top of the door frame.

Levi sat on the edge of his bed, his hands planted firmly and stubbornly on his knees. He looked safe and unharmed with his coat buttoned up to the collar and his felt hat on his head. Luke noticed a hammer on the floor between his bare feet. The curved, yellowing toenails made Luke wonder how well his father was caring for himself. He hoped their sudden move had not caused a more dramatic internal change. Levi obviously had more than one issue. Luke wondered for a moment why the man would be dressed completely except for his feet.

"We will have to come back to repair the hydraulics," stated the older *Englische*, distracting Luke's thoughts.

The mention of the broken door gave Luke an idea, but not about footwear. He said, "May I suggest, instead of repairing the mechanics that you mount a handle? That way, the door can be opened or closed manually."

The two Englische looked at each other and shrugged. The older one said, "We would have to take the whole door system offline for your quarters. All of the doors would be manual, but everything else would stay the same."

Luke looked to his father, but Levi still did not move. Then Luke turned to Annie. Her eyes told a whole story and almost showed a glint of approval. For the first time in a week, he might do something to make his wife happy. Luke said to the Englische, "As it should be. If we cannot access our world by our own hand, then it truly is not our world. Please take offline this system."

Ideally, Luke would have asked for them to cut off the electricity to their entire quarters. He decided not to ask because he knew the ship was not designed that way. The *Englische* relied on electricity and technology as much as they relied on oxygen. It had been a part of their lives for hundreds of years and seemed it would continue to evolve.

Once the Englische left to get the tools and supplies they needed for the door system, Luke entered his father's room. He stepped through the door sideways to avoid the still dripping purple hydraulic fluid. He stood over Levi in the same way he would stand over one of his own children who had misbehaved.

"You do not ask permission to enter my private room?" snipped Levi.

Luke felt a sudden sting at forgetting his manners. He instantly justified his position, looking down at the hammer on the floor. Back by the door, Luke saw exposed wires and a broken computer screen. Even though this was his father, Luke was the head of this household. He took responsibility for everyone and everything in these quarters. If someone under his care had a transgression, regardless of proper manners, Luke had to address it.

His train of thought carried him around to the children watching from the next room. Luke decided it best not to speak harshly toward his father. He did not want to set an example that could come visit him some day. He knew it was not the child's place to discipline the parent. Luke took a different approach.

"Where did you get the hammer, *Daed*?"

Levi's head seemed to drop a little lower. His salt and pepper beard bunched up against his chest.

Luke did not think he was going to answer, but then the old man said, "I brought it with me."

They had no possessions. They lost everything in the tornadoes. Luke scanned his father's room. Maybe in all the excitement he had not noticed that Levi carried his own suitcase. To Luke's surprise, the tattered case with worn hinges sat open in the corner. There looked to be a few shirts, but he could not see what caused the bulges beneath the shirts. He would keep his curiosity at bay for now.

Luke bent and picked up the hammer. He could feel the ventilation on his hand coming up through the slotted floor as his fingers curled around the wooden handle. He thought that the constant flow of air could not be good for bare feet. He would have to remember to discuss that with Annie later. Old men and children could easily catch a cold walking with bare feet on this unfriendly metal floor.

Examining the hammer, Luke sat next to his father on the edge of the bed. He asked, "Why would you bring a hammer on a spaceship?"

For the first time, Levi made eye contact with Luke. Luke saw a mix of anger and sadness in his father's eyes. Levi answered with his own question, "Did I know we were coming to a spaceship?"

His father was right. Luke did not have an answer for that. He worked hard to keep their destination a secret, going so far as skipping church twice. He reasoned with his family that the increasing storms kept them from going. They held their own church and had almost no contact with anyone the month before they left. Luke wanted to say something to his father. Instead, they sat in silence.

Luke's thoughts turned to the day he made the decision to save their lives...

******

The dust storms had been increasing. Luke heard of a few tornadoes striking nearby towns. With failing crops, Luke started making a weekly trip for food and supplies. The Bishop had the forethought to distribute some monies the church earned through selling various goods and services in the past. Normally, they did not have much use for *Englische* dollars. The savings had grown quite a bit with no use. Now that they needed it for basic survival, the Bishop found use for the money.

On one return trip on the normally lonely stretch of country road, Luke saw the *Englische* putting up a chain link fence. Behind the fence, the men constructed two rows of temporary buildings. The sign above the wide gate read *Corinthian Port*. This made no sense to Luke. They were miles away from the closest river or any boats. He wondered what kind of port they could be building.

A thunderous roar startled him. It sounded as if the sky split open and a concussive blast almost knocked Luke from the bench of his wagon. He felt Earl yank at the reins. Had the poor horse been in better health, he might have pulled free from his harness out of panic. Luke expected this kind of sound when the Host returned for the Rapture. Years of good Amish living prepared him for that day, but he suddenly had a hint of doubt in the back of his mind. What if he was not ready?

The sound seemed to come from the sky in answer to his question about the port. The other questions would have to wait. Luke looked up into the pale yellow clouds that he actually started to grow used to. Something that he could only describe as a big metal box pushed through the clouds and landed with a thud back behind the new fence. Luke had been on an airplane once, in his youth, and knew of the International Space Program. He even heard of private *Englische* companies building their own spaceships, offering once in a lifetime experiences for those that could afford it. This was the first time Luke saw a spaceship up close and it did not impress him.

The non-descript transport seemed more suited for carrying cargo. It reminded him of the large metal containers that might be on a cargo ship at sea. Except, he thought, this looked twice as wide as one of those and maybe a little longer. As he sat pondering, three more dropped out of the sky. Each landed equally as rough as the first. Suddenly, Luke spotted rows of these vehicles. They had been sitting there this whole time, back behind the fence, obscured by the dingy haze. There had to be at least thirty of them, but he guessed it to be closer to fifty.

Luke felt the overwhelming need to understand what he was seeing. The *Englische* workers looked too busy to talk, but someone had to be in charge. Luke guided Earl away from the gate and found a short fence to hitch him to. The split rail marked the edge of somebody's property, but, at the moment, Luke could not recall which neighbor it was. Earl had always been a good horse and a hard worker. Luke felt bad for letting his health diminish. Sadly, it came to a choice of feeding his family or feeding his animals. Luke suspected it would get worse. He could already see Earl's ribs pressing against his dusty brown coat.

He headed through the gate, under the Corinthian Port sign. It looked like there was a booth for a guard, but it stood empty. No one stopped Luke from entering the new port. The temporary buildings on either side looked like shops. On his left, a technician was attaching a computer monitor to the wall of what appeared to be a newsstand. Luke thought he might get some information there, but then he spied another building. The wind-whipped shingle hanging over the stoop read *Port Authority*.

That had to be the place, he thought. As Luke headed toward the building, he realized something. He realized that he did not feel out of place surrounded by all of this *Englische*. He had plenty of dealings with them and tolerated the *Neufremdefreunds*, the Englische converts. While he never used any, computers and electronics were no stranger to him. He suddenly thought maybe God intended for him to be here this day. Maybe the good Lord shielded him from the temptation and delivered him to some possible salvation. He did not know what was happening to his world, but he thought that a change might be coming.

Luke took three steps up to the small stoop outside the door to the Port Authority. He reached for the door handle and uncontrollably held his breath. He thought for a moment that going through this door would change his life forever. He did not know what to expect, but worried that he would have to surrender part of himself to cross the threshold. He reassured himself that as long as he had faith in his God, it did not matter what else he had to give up to find salvation. He felt that a change might be necessary.

He opened the door.

The strange effect of noisy wind instantly silenced caught Luke every time. These days, the wind blew constantly. Still, Luke noticed how quiet it got each time he went inside his house, his barn, or wherever. The three *Englische* inside the Port Authority noticed him too. The gust of wind and noise drew their attention to the door as Luke pulled it closed. One of the men sat behind a squat metal desk. The other two sat on a bench along the wall as if they were waiting for something or simply visiting. Luke removed his hat. These days, he had a harder and harder time keeping it on while outside.

"Good day, gentlemen," offered Luke.

"You sure about that?" said one of the men on the bench. A toothy, smug smile on his pudgy face told Luke that he probably liked to tease. Men like this found delight in mocking the Amish. The man either did not understand the Amish or did not have his own beliefs.

Luke did his best to ignore the man, but the other *Englische* on the bench got a little laugh from the comment. Luke turned his attention to the man behind the desk. He looked cut from stone with a square head and square shoulders. Luke knew he was not, but the man seemed as wide as the desk. This appeared to be the sort of man that worked hard his entire life. His only reward, in this life, came in the form of a title and small desk in a small construction trailer. Maybe he had nothing more to look forward to, but at least he did not spend his time toiling in this unpleasant weather.

Before Luke could say anything, the man with the Authority title said, "Sign on the bottom line."

Looking where the man pointed, Luke saw a stack of papers on the edge of the desk closest to him. It appeared to be some kind of contract, probably a hundred of them, pre-prepared.

"What is this?" Luke asked.

The Authority looked perturbed. He said, "Are you here to sign for your place?"

Luke felt lost. The confidence he had outside faltered. He worried for a moment that these *Englische* were trying to trick him into doing something, maybe signing away his fields. "For what place am I signing?"

"It doesn't matter. You don't have to sign. Have your family here at the designated time and we will take you. You're not the only one that refused to sign," said the Authority.

Luke truly did not understand. He was not about to sign a contract with the *Englische*. For all he knew, they caused this situation and now, through trickery, they were trying to get out of it. It seemed bold of them to want to take the Amish away. What could they do with the vacant land, he wondered. It definitely would not be good for growing anything in this weather. It felt as if Luke stood on the edge of the cliff, faced some great temptation.

The pudgy *Englische* said, "Don't you know the world's coming to an end?"

He did know that. He knew, in His own time, that God would bring an end to this and lift up the faithful. It surprised Luke that this *Englische* would speak of that. This pudgy man could not know the truth, as no one knows the day or the hour. Luke said, "I know the storms have been getting worse and most of our crops have failed."

"Don't you watch the news?" asked the Authority.

"We don't own a television," answered Luke. This brought a snort from the pudgy man.

The Authority continued, "Don't any of you Amishes pay attention to the outside world? One of your knights or bishops had to know. They been talking about this for over a year on TV, which means them scientists and governments have pro'ly known about it for five years."

"I'm sorry," said Luke. "My Bishop has told me nothing." In saying this, it occurred to him that visits from the Bishop had been less frequent. They maybe met three times in the past three months. When they did meet, the Bishop seemed unusually quiet in retrospect.

"What he said." The Authority waved a thumb at the pudgy man. "The world is going to end. They called it a climate shift or somethin' like that. I figure Mother Nature is goin' through menopause. Anyhow, it's time to abandon ship. Our boss, Adam Corp, made a deal with the government and you get a free ride. It don't matter to me if you sign the paper or not."

Something turned in Luke's stomach. Had it been any earlier, he might have lost his breakfast. Thankfully, he had time to digest the food, but he would need more time to digest this information. He knew it had become bad, but he never imagined how bad. He never expected a literal end to the world. He said, "Are you asking me to leave my home? My farm? This is our way of life. We cannot run off with you *Englische*."

"I can't say it any other way. You stay, you die." The Authority's expression did not match his words. He did not seem to care either way.

Feeling woozy, Luke said, "I should pray on this. Do you have some place I could go?"

Pudgy piped up, "Oh sure. We got a special booth in the back, right behind that curtain."

Of course, there was no curtain. Luke would be sure to include this man in his prayers. End of the world or not, some people needed extra saving.

The Authority said, "I need a decision today. I have a quota to fill and I can't save the whole world."

Luke felt pressured to make a decision on the spot that he was not even aware of a few minutes ago. He thought about his feelings outside. He had a random thought about salvation and now it seemed he was faced with that very decision. He worried whether to trust the *Englische*. He knew in his heart that God would see them through anything. It should not matter where their feet touch the earth because his Father will always lift their spirits to Heaven.

Then an unfamiliar feeling crept into Luke's heart. He did not recognize it because he almost never felt it. He had a vision of his house torn asunder by a tornado. He saw his wife buried under kitchen rubble. He pictured Katie's wheelchair mangled into a ball and no sign of baby Matthew. Luke always had a vivid imagination. This time, it worked against him. He realized that unfamiliar feeling was fear. Luke could not sit and watch his family die. He knew they would be cradled in God's arms, but he was not ready to release his hold on them.

"If you don't mind, I'll pray right here," said Luke. He glanced sideways to see the smirk fading on Pudgy's face. "Father, please guide my heart and mind. Make me Your willing servant to lead a life that shares Your light and give me the days to do it. I say from the Book of Romans: For I am persuaded, that neither death, nor life, nor angels, nor principalities, nor powers, nor things present, nor things to come, nor height, nor depth, nor any other creature, shall be able to separate us from the love of God, which is in Christ Jesus our Lord."

As he said the words, images of his children's bodies spread across a ragged field impeded his thoughts. He made his decision. If God saw fit to wipe clean the face of His Earth, then Luke Umble would do everything in his power to keep his family from being wiped away with it. He saw no value in a paper contract, but held the *Englische* at their word.

"Where will you take us?" asked Luke. He felt a bead of sweat form on his forehead as he stuck out his hand. He thought a gentleman's handshake would suffice for this deal. If not, God's will win out.

The Authority again displayed his indifference as he pointed toward the ceiling. He said, "Up there, somewhere. Them scientists picked out another planet like Earth." After a quick hand shake, the Authority turned to his computer tablet and tapped the screen with his thick finger. "How many are you?"

"Seven," Luke replied automatically. Then he said, "No, eight." He could not leave his father behind if he was to take his whole family. However, he could already imagine the arguments and the amount of convincing he would have to do with Levi. Then a thought passed through his head like a dark cloud passing in front of the sun. Out in the field, when the cloud left, somehow things always seemed a little brighter. Luke's dark decision was not to tell his family the truth. He certainly would not lie, but, in this case, withholding information would not be the same as a lie. That made the outcome of possible arguments and protests a little brighter. Standing amongst these *Englische*, he rationalized that decision a little too easily for his own liking.

Pudgy actually lifted his girth from the bench. He stepped next to Luke and slapped him on the shoulder. With that obnoxious grin, he said, "Looks like somebody's taking a trip. Glad to see you Amish ain't all alike. The head of the household made a decision without havin' to discuss it in committee."

******

Thinking back to that day, Luke realized the pudgy *Englische* was right about two things. First, they were taking a trip. At the time, Luke had no inclination of how far or how long they would travel. The journey promised more than even Luke's imagination. It would be a true peregrination of Biblical scale.

The second thing that occurred to Luke was that he was the head of the household. He alone made the decision to bring them here. He saved their lives. It was his duty and his responsibility. His father, like his wife and children, would have to submit to his authority.

"Did I know we were coming to a spaceship?" finished Levi in response to Luke's question about the hammer.

Luke gathered his thoughts and finished recounting what brought him to this moment. He said, "But why a hammer? No matter where we were going, what use would be a hammer?"

Levi snagged the hammer by its steel head and pulled it to his chest. He had a look of aggravation, a look with which Luke grew all too familiar. Levi said, "This very hammer I used to build the house in which you were born. My father gave me this tool and it from his father before him. Only once have I replaced the handle. This steel here is as unyielding as the Word of God."

Luke never thought of his father as a sentimental man. So many times they stood at odds with one another. Luke never looked at him simply as a man. He always saw him as a strict and distant father. The loss of Luke's mother obviously changed him. Sometime before that, he must have been a loving, pious man. Luke never understood why his father was so accepting of the *Neufremdefreunds*. Seeing him now seemed to shed a little light on that.

Why would he bring a hammer on a spaceship? He did not bring it as a tool. Luke understood that Levi brought it for what it represented. He looked again at the old suitcase, probably a symbol itself to his father. He wondered what meaning the other artifacts held hidden under those shirts.

Luke's heart softened a little. He could not punish Levi as he would Henry for such behavior. All the same, he was in charge and could not allow that behavior. The *Englische* crewmen would return soon to fix all of the doors.

He said, "*Daed*, I know you're scared. We all are."

"I'm not scared," interrupted Levi. "I am betrayed by my own child. You admit you are scared and I see you have acted out of fear. Through your own weakness, you have dragged your family into something that even you don't understand."

"It is always the same with you," started Luke. He felt that his father would never let him stand on his own, never respect his decisions. "How many times do I have to say that I saved you? I saved my wife and children. I was…I am scared, but I do not act out of fear. My heart and mind are in accord. I have faith that we will have a new life. If I hadn't dragged you from the house you built, you'd be dead."

Levi stood. He said, "But then I would be truly saved. You say you saved our lives. This flesh does not concern me." He pinched the wrinkled skin on the back of his own hand. "Only God in Heaven can save me. My soul is not yours to horde like a spoiled child."

That hard man came back. The affection Luke momentarily felt for the man faded into the uneasy relationship between father and son. Luke could not bring himself to continue the discussion. He did not know how to make his father understand. He said, "This is our life now. If you continue to mistreat the *Englische* machines, I will have to ask them to find you separate quarters."

Luke did not wait for a response. He left the room, not attempting to dodge the leaking hydraulic fluid. Purple liquid splashed on the shoulder of his sweat-stained white work shirt and ran down the front of his suspenders. Annie reached for him, but he walked past her toward their bedroom. He wanted to be alone.

Before he reached his bedroom door, he realized that his wife was trying to comfort him. Their relationship had been strained of late. Turning away from her now would only make things worse. He held out his hand and Annie came to him. Together, they went into the bedroom for prayer and solitude.

Four

Revelation

For as many people that were on the *Corinthian*, the halls seemed unusually empty. Katie Umble did not mind it so much. Wheeling back to their family quarters after school, she liked the alone time.

In fact, she needed it.

Katie had been in the wheelchair for almost two years. Because of their beliefs, her father would only allow a manual chair. She never told him that she wished for an automated wheelchair. She once saw one with special wheels for climbing stairs and its own wireless internet connection. So many of the Amish started using the internet once U.S. currency converted to digital thumbprints back in the year 2050. Katie wished she could try it. Again, her father said no.

At the new school on board the space ship, they were required to use computers for reading and math. The Wi-Fi tablet could access information from anywhere on the ship. Katie carefully tucked it away in the special pouch her mother sewed and slung over her right armrest. She did not dare take it out in front of her parents or grandfather. Only when she was sure Henry was asleep, would she sneak a peek, looking at places on Earth she would never go or reading books about girls that could walk and have adventures.

"My ugly legs," Katie muttered. No one heard her in the long brown hall. That is why she liked the solitude. Since the onset of the Muscular Dystrophy, she had gotten used to her thick, clumsy calves. When she turned ten, with almost no strength in her legs, she started using the wheelchair. She had gotten used to that too.

On board this ship, she discovered that the other kids were not used to it. They excluded her from activities and some even teased her. When they went to the recreation hall, they simply ignored her. It bothered her more that back on Earth she went to school with some of these kids. They already knew her and were not mean back then. Some of these new kids, she learned had gone to an Englische school, where bullying was a problem. It made her sad that the Amish children who were once bullied now became the bullies. She heard her mother say on many occasions, "Kids will be kids." Katie did not think she meant that teasing and name-calling was okay. She must have meant that kids will behave how they can until an adult corrects them.

Katie wanted to ask for help from her teacher, but they only had three teachers for all of Level Eight. The poor women could barely control the children long enough for their lessons. They did not have time for anything beyond that. So Katie dealt with her emotional pain on her own, the same as she dealt with her physical pain.

Alone.

Alone, but not sad. She had nothing but joy for her life. The doctors told her all of the bad things, but

God spoke only good. Her body may betray her. Her muscles will eventually break down. For now, God gave her strong arms, on her best days, to push herself. He gave her an understanding heart and a keen mind. She loved life and intended to make the best of every minute the good Lord bestowed on her in this life.

Some nights, she laid in bed, concentrating on her breathing. She would not tell her parents that her lungs felt more pressure on board the Corinthian. She did not want to steal what little hope they had left. When she took one breath in and forced it back out, in those late hours, she would pray. In those prayers, she heard a soft voice. It was a quiet, soothing sound, not booming or commanding. This voice felt like a warm blanket wrapped tightly around her, snug, like her mother wrapped her when she was a baby. Katie listened for the voice.

It said, "Be his anchor."

On this lonely journey from school to home, Katie recounted those words. Since she first heard it two nights ago, she thought about it a lot. Whose anchor, she asked herself. "My father's?" she said aloud. Katie peered over her shoulder. Nothing but the brown metal walls and the dull yellow lights shining out from their hiding places. No one heard her talking to herself. Good, she thought, she did not want to give her classmates anymore reason to tease her.

No matter how much she asked, the voice did not come back. She only had those three little words. Three. Like the Trinity, she thought. Somehow, she understood that God was with them. They did not leave Him behind on Earth. They were not drifting alone in space. She realized that they were connected to God through their hearts. As long as they honored

Him and held His place in their hearts, He would be there. Katie felt proud of herself for coming to that understanding.

Then it happened. Her left wheel slipped into a groove between two plates. She did not have the strength to roll out of it. Katie could not move her chair. She knew instantly that this was payment for her prideful boasting. She pretended for a minute that she knew God's plan and he sent her a reminder. She was not truly alone in this corridor. Obviously, if she was, she would have gotten stuck much sooner. God must have been guiding her wheels each previous time she left school. Letting her get stuck showed her what it might truly be like to be alone.

"Papa," Katie called. She could only yell one more time without her lungs starting to burn. She could call for her brothers or maybe one of the teachers. She doubted anyone could hear her. Even her mother would be too far away, especially with their front door closed. She called again, "Papa, I'm stuck."

Her lungs flared. She could do no more than whisper now. Still, she knew her father would come. Fathers always knew when their daughters needed them. Many people would curse their position at this point. They would be angry at their failing bodies or, possibly, even go so far as to blame God. Katie did none of that. She sat in her chair and concentrated on her breathing. Each breath felt like rolling herself up a steep hill. She only wanted to close her eyes and rest. She did and the dim yellow turned to black.

The sound of heavy boots clomping on the metal floor woke her. Katie had no idea how long she slept. It must have been quite a while because she could not feel any burning in her lungs. The pain had subsided for now. The person approached from behind and she could not turn far enough to see who it was.

She did not have to. As soon as Luke Umble put his arms around his daughter, she knew. Only one person could make her feel that safe. Her father moved and knelt in front of her. John appeared behind him. She knew her brother and father had been having disagreements lately. It made her feel good that they could still come together on some things.

"You had us so worried. I came home from the field and you were not there," he said. His eyes seemed filled with tears, but they would not drop to his cheeks.

"It's not like I could get lost. Where would I go?" Katie joked. She tried to laugh away her own tears.

"Come, let us get you home," said her father. Luke struggled with the chair. He seemed to be having difficulty pulling her loose. He said, "You are anchored in, but good."

Anchored. Her father said the same word she heard in her prayer. Or was it a dream? Either way, she knew now for whom she was supposed to be an anchor. The doctors told her eventually her lungs would stop working like her legs. She would not tell her parents that it already started. God had a purpose for her and she would not go anywhere until she fulfilled that purpose.

******

After Katie's incident in the hall, she confided one thing in her parents. She told them about the bullying. Mary did not like seeing her younger sister treated this way. She wanted to help Katie and told her parents so.

77

"I want to go to school with Katie," she volunteered.

Their mother said, "You have already finished your schooling. What would you do?"

"I could keep her safe," said Mary.

"You cannot be by her side your whole life," said Annie.

Annie studied her. Mary could almost feel her thoughts as her mother scanned her up and down. Mary led an obedient life and on every subject, her parents had the final word. She followed dutifully. That was her old life, the sixteen years spent on Earth. They had a new life now and Mary did something she never imagined she would do.

She challenged her mother.

"I…" Mary hesitated. "I think I should be there."

Her mother gasped. The pan she held clanged hard on the counter. The woman did not completely lose her temper. Mary had never seen that. Still, she could feel some retribution coming. First John showed his independence, and now Mary spoke against her mother's wishes. She knew this would not be tolerated in the Umble house. Mary did not want to disobey her mother, but at the same time she wanted to help her sister.

Before Annie could respond to her daughter, Katie rolled to the kitchen doorway. Mary guessed the clever girl had been listening from the next room. Katie said, "You know, we only have three teachers on our level. I heard that some levels have six or seven."

Katie said nothing else. Mary looked from her sister to her mother. Annie did not look as flustered as she did a moment ago. She turned away from her daughters and delivered the recently washed pan to its proper cabinet. Mary already had an idea, but she waited for her mother to say it.

Annie said, "Go with your sister in the morning. Ask if they need a teacher's assistant. You will be well suited for it. You can see that Katie gets home without becoming stuck alone again. Besides, there will be plenty of time for your chores after supper."

Annie rested her hands on her hips as she looked at her daughters. She twisted her mouth like she might be biting the inside of her cheek. Mary stole a glance at Katie, still in the doorway. She could see a hint of a smile twinkling in her sister's eyes. This would be good for both of them. Mary intended to watch out for her sister, but it would also be the first opportunity she had to stand on her own.

After all, she was almost a woman. It would not be long until baptism and then she would turn her mind to finding a husband. Mary had not met anyone her age on board the ship yet, boy or girl. She loved her mother, but desperately wanted some new company. She barely left their quarters since they arrived. Maybe some of her new students would have older brothers or sisters, she hoped. That is, of course, if they allowed her to be a teacher's assistant. She had no idea what would be expected of her and even less of an idea why her mother thought she was well suited.

"Now get ready your Sunday dress. You will need to be properly dressed. It won't be much time and I will be making supper. When your father comes home, I will tell him of our decision," said Annie.

Mary liked that her mother said *our decision*. She felt like a young woman, an equal.

******

For the second time in two nights, John joined them for supper. He missed his family, but enjoyed his newfound independence. His father did not approve of John working closely with the *Englische* and that put them at odds. Instead of talking and dealing with their feelings, Luke ignored the problem and pretended everything was fine.

That seemed like an Amish thing to do, thought John. He heard his father talking with his mother many times over the years about how his grandfather shut out the rest of the world. From John's point of view, it seemed like the Amish perfected a way of pretending the rest of the world did not exist. At least, that's how he saw Luke and Levi Umble. John saw a son trying so hard not to be like his father, yet he was becoming the same man.

John knew not all Amish were like this, but it became easier for him to stay away. Now that his grandfather lived with them, John could feel the tension between them mounting. He wanted to talk to someone about this and most times, it ended up being Huxtable in Engineering. He liked talking to Hux, though. When they were alone together, it felt like they had been friends for years. In front of the other engineers, she was definitely in charge.

The chief engineer seemed to like hearing about his family, but John noticed that she never offered any advice. Maybe he only needed someone to voice his feelings to. Then he could try to figure things out on his own. The real struggle came with the things she did say. Hux taught John about engineering and he had no problem learning the mechanics of his new job. He had a problem with the information that came with it.

Hux told him things about the ship that she said her bosses would prefer to remain secret.

Sitting at the dinner table, John contemplated sharing the troubling news with his family. At the moment, they all looked happy to be together. Even his grandfather did not have a scowl. He did not smile, but at least no scowl. They gave thanks and shared a meal as a family. John did not want to ruin the moment. He worried what might come of them if he did not tell. Still, Hux had spoken to him in confidence.

John thought back to their conversation. She finished showing him how to backwash the potable filters. They were alone in a small room, accessible only by a narrow, pipe-crowded corridor. The engine room felt like a maze made worse by being three levels instead of one. Hux stopped after she turned one of the valves. John thought she looked on the verge of tears.

"Have you thought about it?"

He had no idea. Was she testing him on his newly gained knowledge?

"I mean have you really thought about this thing we're doing?" she asked again.

John assumed she meant something bigger than the filter cleaning. Maybe he missed some instruction. Part of his problem in learning the new job was that he usually only concentrated on how pretty the chief engineer was. He anticipated times when they would be alone. Now that they were so secluded, he imagined himself kissing her. In his daydream, he must have missed something that led to her question.

She must not have shared the same thoughts. She said, "This ship has a passenger capacity of ten thousand, not counting the crew. I suppose you couldn't really count most of them anyway. The final evacuations were so chaotic that we only have about seven thousand on board."

John started to understand what she meant. She apparently wanted to process some thoughts that weighed heavy on her.

"Now think about it," she continued. "Sixteen ships and maybe two of them were loaded properly and in advance. That means only two of them were boarded to capacity. Even if they were full, that is sixteen ships multiplied by ten thousand people. Less than one hundred and sixty thousand people made it off the planet. In a way, we sentenced several billion people to death."

Hux buried her head into John's chest. He could feel her body move against his as she sobbed. He had not expected such an emotional display from her. In the few days he had known her, she showed herself to be strong and confident. This mood came as a surprising reveal. John put his arms around her, partly for selfish reasons. John thought about what she said. The Earth was dying and the Adam Corp ships were open to anyone that wanted to go. He felt like everyone had a choice.

"We can't be responsible for those that did not want to leave," he told her.

She looked up at him with tears streaking over her greasy cheeks. She said, "I appreciate you trying to make me feel better, but I can't help feeling guilty. When I took this job, I was not even allowed to tell my family. They lived in Tampa before the Florida quake. The house I grew up in is under a hundred feet of water now and I lost my parents."

John could not understand how she could speak so casually about this. He understood her feeling of guilt. If Adam Corp would not allow her to warn her family, what other dishonest things did they do?

"The world was coming apart. It's not your fault," said John. He tried to comfort her, but she pulled away.

She wiped her eyes with the backs of her gloves. Her vulnerability faded. She said, "I have to stay focused. We have other concerns."

"Like what?" asked John. His emotions swayed with hers. He barely had time to think about all of the people left behind on that dying planet.

"Water consumption is off the chart," she answered. "No one anticipated how resistant you Amish would be to using our systems. Instead of the laundry efficiencies, too many are washing clothes in the sink and hand washing dishes. Potable water is being used at a rate that exceeds the filtration process."

John really did not know, so he asked, "What does that mean?"

Hux switched back fully to her chief mode. She said, "What does that mean? It means if we don't find a planet with water in less than a year, we won't need a planet. Don't you understand we are going to run out of water?"

He understood it now. He thought about the three million gallons of water held in the massive tank that took up most of the space in engineering. Three million seemed like an unbelievable amount. It seemed like it would last forever. The way Hux explained it, she made it seem like they almost had none.

"I know I'm putting a lot on you, but I had to tell someone. I think it is the price we have to pay for leaving all those people behind. But it gets worse," she said.

How could it be worse, wondered John. He did not have to ask.

Huxtable explained, "Even at top speed, the VASIMR engine will only travel about one tenth of light speed. That's faster than anything I've ever worked on, but it's not fast enough. Unless those big brains upstairs find an alternate planet, we will never make it. Assuming we could not use all of our cooling water, at our best speed, it is going to take six hundred years to reach JER-29.11."

John felt a flush of outrage. His family gave up everything for a chance at salvation that Hux now tells him may never come. He felt emotions that never occurred to him in his plain life. His father had been tricked and lied to. He asked, "Does the captain know any of this?"

"It's not his job. He's in charge of publicity and morale. I suspect the scientists do and that is why they are desperately searching for a closer option. I tried to express concern to my boss back at Adam Corp, but I was told if I said anything that I would be put on ground crew and left behind."

"We should say something now," started John. He almost ran from the compartment. His first thought was to go to his father.

Hux grabbed his arm. Despite the revelations she shared, he liked her touch. She said, "What good would it do? We have nowhere to go and it would probably start a ship-wide panic. At least there is peace for now."

Peace for now.

John looked around the table at the faces of his family. They did seem to be enjoying some peace. No one argued. No one looked scared. They had only been away from Earth about two weeks, but he felt like this had been their home for a long time. He did not want to upset that peace.

At the end of the meal, before the children asked to be excused, John's father asked for everyone's attention. Luke said, "Family, I have a concern and since it affects us all, I will present it to you all."

John watched his mother take his father's hand. They both looked a little worried. Luke continued, "I fear the *Englische* are mis-managing the crops. They are exposing the young plants to too much sunlight and not enough water. I have already seen some wilting. If it continues, we will not have nearly enough yield. What I have learned from some of the other men is that we are the only ship using traditional planting. All of the other vessels are using hydroponics."

"What are hydra-fonics?" asked Henry. This brought a chuckle from their father and a weak, forced-looking smile from their mother.

"It is a different way of farming, without the use of God's own earth, but that is not what's important. The concern is that if we have a short crop, then we will go through all of the food stores. The plan was to use the previously stored food until the crops came in, then we would be self-sustaining. I have prayed about how to solve this and I feel that you, my family, will help guide me."

With that news, John watched the peace and happiness slip from his families' faces. Where there was care free a moment ago, he now saw concern and hints of worry. He knew for sure that he would not share his news now. The problems with the water and engine would only make things worse. He felt it would be better to deal with one thing at a time and let his father head the way.

"What say you, family? Do I go speak to Captain Nixon or do I work the soil and make the most of what God has blessed us with?" asked Luke.

Levi Umble spoke first. He said, "A man should provide for his family. You have assumed the responsibility of carrying us through this void. It is your responsibility to work the crops. What would you do on Earth if there was a drought? Treat this as the same. The *Englische* will come around when the problem is revealed."

It did not surprise John that his grandfather felt this way, but it did disappoint him. Obviously, if his father did not act to change things now, it would be too late to change them for the next crop. John worked alongside his father long enough to know that they would lose valuable nutrients and precious time if they let this crop wither.

"Want me to go with you, Pa?" proposed John as a way of casting his vote to speak with the captain. He also thought maybe he could share some of his dreadful knowledge. Maybe the combination of impending troubles would help Captain Nixon recognize their dire situation.

Luke stood from the table. He said, "No. I should speak with him man to man. You have chosen different labor and the field is my responsibility, as your grandfather said. Besides, I think many of the men look up to me. I will be the best representative for this."

John felt like he could see his father actually rising up over the table. He knew his decision to work in the engine room drove a wedge between them. He could see now his father's pride widened that gap. Growing up, John always saw his father walking a different path, but he believed it was a path that God laid before him. The course he took now seemed to be of his own choosing. If Luke Umble believed he was the leader of Amish men on this ship, then John could offer nothing more. If, and when, his father fell from that lofty place, John intended to be there to pick him up and stand beside him. He knew he was not a bad son and he meant no disrespect to their beliefs. He wanted to be his own man and use the gift God gave him in the way he knew how.

By the time his mother and sister cleared the table, everyone except Levi supported Luke's decision to go talk to the captain. John knew that his father always respected his mother's opinion. However, he knew that his sister Katie was often instrumental in his father's decision making. Everybody, including John, recognized something special in the wheel-chair bound girl. Maybe it has to do with her disease, but he did not think so. John felt that his sister had been touched by the Holy Spirit. When Katie agreed to the plan, it was no longer open to discussion.

John kept his bad news to himself and went to bed early. He would be off to work that much earlier the next day. He would tell Hux about the problems with the crops and see if that would not change her mind about sharing her news.

******

87

The first day of school. The very thought gives some people bad dreams. Mary did not sleep enough to have any dreams. The thought of going back to school kept her awake almost all night. Of course, Mary would not be a student. She completed eighth grade long before they left Earth. She was going to ask for a job. Her mother said she would be suited to be a teacher's assistant and according to her sister Katie, they needed the help.

After some prayer and quiet contemplation, Mary decided her best choice would be to focus on scripture and reminding the children of their behavior. The three teachers on Level Eight were all *Englische* crewmembers. Mary intended to let them worry about the computers. She was not ready to learn something like that, although she watched Katie some nights flipping through pictures on her tablet. She pretended to be asleep when her sister snuck out the portable computer.

Wheeling Katie down the hall in the morning, Mary heard something she never expected. Laughing and yelling. The raucous sound grew louder each time the door opened and a student entered. Mary noticed that the children walked to school unattended. Why not, she asked herself. They could not get lost and had no worry of a random stranger causing problems or worse. The kids were safe to walk to school on their own.

Inside the classroom, which very much resembled their quarters, except on a much larger scale, the kids were out of control. Mary could not believe the behaviors she witnessed. The boys pulled girls' pony tails. They played tag and ran about the room. She expected to see paper airplanes, but they had no paper.

Mary could barely find the teacher. She found her at the back end of the room, dressed in the blue coveralls of any other crewmember. This lady bore a striking resemblance to their tour guide, Mindi. It had been several days since Mary last saw Mindi and, at first, thought it was her.

"Hi, I'm Mary Umble, Katie's sister," offered Mary with a polite handshake.

The teacher did not take her hand. A blank look fell across her face for a moment. Then, as if Katie was not sitting right next to them, she said, "Yes, Katie Umble. Superior student. High aptitude. Muscular Dystrophy. She is one of my students. I am designated 1T212. The students refer to me as Moira."

Mary dropped her hand and said, "Miss Moira..."

"No," interrupted Moira, "they do not call me Miss."

Mary thought it strange that the children would not show their teacher the simple respect of calling her Miss. Looking around the room, it appeared the students had no respect whatsoever. Mary insisted on maintaining her manners. She said, "Miss Moira, my mother suggested that I ask you if you are in need of a teacher's assistant. She wants me to have some work outside of my home chores. Would it be okay if I worked with you?"

That blank stare came back to Moira's face. Mary noticed this with Mindi too. It is almost like they were concentrating hard on something. Moira's eyes refocused on Mary. The teacher said, "I see nothing in the ship ordinances that would forbid it. Yes, please assist me." Moira turned to address the class. "Children, it is time to begin today's lesson."

Almost none of the students acknowledged her. "Children, please," repeated Moira in a soft, level voice. Mary assumed the kids thought they were on some kind of vacation. She stuck the pinky finger from each hand in the corners of her mouth. A second before she issued a piercing whistle, Katie slapped her hands over her ears. Mary learned the trick from their father and Katie never could duplicate it, but she knew when it was coming. Every child froze, silent, their eyes on Mary.

"I don't know what behavior I am seeing here, but I definitely think your parents would be disappointed. It would be a shame if I had to escort each of you home with a bad report. You are Amish children and this foolishness will not be tolerated. I want to see respect for your teacher and each other starting now. I am Miss Mary and you will call your teacher *Miss* Moira. Now take your seats." The children quietly moved to their seats. Mary heard one or two whispers to the effect that they would not want to make her angry.

When eyes were off of her and facing the front of the classroom, Mary took a deep breath. She could not believe she did what she did. It was not like her to be so authoritative or be the center of attention. It seemed to come natural and she understood a little better why her mother thought she would be well suited for the job.

Shortly after Miss Moira began the lesson, a young man escorted a boy into the classroom. Mary moved to meet them at the door.

The young man said, "Sorry we're late."

"It's okay," said Mary. She looked at both of the newcomers. They shared similar dark features: a heavy, but not dull, brow; shiny black hair; and thin lips. The younger was clearly related to the older. Mary said, "It is nice to see a parent involved in their child's education."

The young man, probably about twenty years old, looked surprised. He said, "Oh, I'm not his dad. This is my kid brother Pete. I'm Nick."

Miss Moira interrupted, "Lieutenant Lincoln, thank you for ensuring Peter's arrival. Will that be all?"

Nick did not dress in the blue coveralls of the crew. Since Miss Moira called him Lieutenant, she understood that he was not Amish, no matter what he was. Nick smiled in a way that made Mary forget about the room full of kids watching them. He said, "Sorry, I have to get to the bridge. I have a meeting with the captain and one of the farmers."

As Mary looked into his eyes, she did not process that he was on the way to meet her father. He looked too young to be in charge of anything. She wanted to talk more with him, but he left without a goodbye. A few snickers brought Mary's attention back to the class. Miss Moira continued the lesson.

Mary helped Peter find a seat and then she sat at the back of the classroom. She found it easy to slip into old habits. Too many times during her school days, the teacher called her out for daydreaming. She did not have the desire to read or study like her younger sister. Maybe she found something she was good at, maybe she could be a better teacher than a student. In the meantime, she let her mind wander to the dashing Lieutenant Nick Lincoln and her hopes of talking to him again.

Five

Downfall

Luke Umble made his way to the command deck. After almost two months on board the Corinthian, he still felt like he was in a maze. The long, dark halls ended in confusing junctions and the claustrophobic elevators pressed in on him. For some reason, the spaceship seemed less crowded with more people around him. Luke liked to walk the halls with his family or friends. The company seemed to bring more light than the hidden yellow bulbs behind the brown metal grates.

He thought he had an appointment to meet with the Captain. It had been a long time coming, but Luke felt like it was his duty. He felt like the spokesman for his people. He knew of at least four bishops on board, but one of them went into hysterics as soon as he came onto the ship. The other three kept their peace and said nothing. Luke felt like God put him in this role. He would be the best leader he could be.

During a previous discussion, his bishop, the one that had visited his house and led their church services, reminded Luke of his place.

"Pride is man's downfall," said the bishop.

"Is it pride to protect your family or feed your people?" asked Luke.

The bishop's eyes seemed to cut through him. Luke knew the bishop was not used to anyone challenging his authority. Back on Earth, the old man had the final say and interpreted the scripture for them. Luke believed they were entitled to a new way of life in this new environment. Part of that new way included new leaders. He believed he was chosen for it and the Lord placed him at the front of his people.

For that reason, he now entered the bridge.

"Captain," called Luke. "Captain Nixon, may I have a word?"

"You're on the wrong deck, Amish," snapped the Captain without looking up from his monitor.

Luke stopped short. The last time he met the Captain, he seemed like a friendly person, shaking hands and smiling. This response belied an entirely different man. Luke knew this was an *Englische* ship, but he had not felt such hostility as he did in the Captain's words at this moment.

"Yes, I am Amish, but the difference in our ideologies is not why I am here," said Luke. He would not let the man's rude behavior turn him away. "I have come to see you, so I believe I am on the correct deck."

The Captain stood. Luke assumed that the man thought showing off his height would be a deterrent. As David stood before Goliath, Luke would not falter. He did not think this was such a conflict, but he steeled himself against any reproach the Captain might offer.

"This is my ship, my bridge. You don't see me down in the fields or the lower decks. Any issues you have should be handled through your deck supervisor. I don't have time for this," said Captain Nixon.

The man reeked of ill temper. Either he truly did not like the Amish, Luke thought, or something else troubled him. Whatever the case, Luke bore the brunt of it.

"I tried to make an appointment with my deck supervisor. Did he not tell you? Let me ask, do you have time for everyone on this ship to starve?" asked Luke. He noticed he caught the attention of a few other people at nearby desks and consoles. He did not want to embellish, but he needed the Captain to hear him.

"What's he talking about, Cap?" said a young man, approaching them from the elevator.

The Captain kept his eyes on Luke. He said, "You're late Lincoln."

Lincoln froze in his tracks and stood at attention. He did not salute, but said, "Sorry, Sir. I had to take Pete to school."

"Handle your family business on your own time. This Amish here seems to think we are all on the verge of starvation. I don't even know how he got in here," said the Captain.

"He scheduled a meeting. I intended to handle it, Sir," said Lincoln.

Captain Nixon turned his back on both of them. He looked across the bridge toward the big viewing window. Luke looked with him and saw nothing but empty space. The stars seemed so far apart now that they were out among them.

The Captain said, "Then handle it. Huxtable is giving me enough to deal with."

The young man put his hand on Luke's shoulder. He led him away from the Captain's desk. "I'm Nick

Lincoln, First Lieutenant. I will be happy to listen to your concerns."

Luke thought Nick Lincoln could not have been much older than his own son John. He felt unsure about trusting such an important matter to a young person. Still, if the *Englische* appointed him to the position, he must have some merit.

Seated at his desk, a much smaller version of the Captain's, Lt. Lincoln looked sincere. He said, "Now, what is this about people starving? That's one of the reasons we left Earth in the first place."

Luke had to concentrate. The actions of Captain Nixon had him distracted. He felt a need to say something more, maybe lecture him like he might his young son Henry. If the Captain wanted to call names and be unpleasant, then maybe he needed to be treated like a child. If anyone could discipline the Captain, Luke believed he could do it.

Instead of saying anything, Luke decided to pray for the man when he next had the opportunity. After all, he had bigger concerns. The whole encounter threw Luke off his course of action. He also heard the Captain mention the Engineer's name. He asked Lincoln, "Was he speaking of Huxtable in engineering? I believe my son works with her."

"That is possible. What's your son's name?" asked the eager Lieutenant.

"John Umble."

Nick Lincoln perked up at the mention of their family name. He said, "I met a Mary Umble this morning in my brother's classroom."

For the first time, Lincoln had Luke's full attention. His daughter was only sixteen and did not yet need any young men taking an interest in her. He could not decide if Lincoln's age bothered him more or the fact that he was *Englische*. Luke read the Lieutenant's expression. He could see the sparkle in his eyes as if he was thinking of Mary right then.

"Before you get any ideas, Mary is not ready for courtship. Don't you think you are too old for those considerations?" asked Luke.

The smile dropped from Lincoln's face instantly. He looked a little confused and embarrassed. He said, "Mr. Umble, I'm sorry. I didn't...I'm not that old. Nineteen, if that helps. I apologize if you think I had any designs on your daughter."

Luke felt some genuine amusement for the first time in a while. He could see how nervous he made the young Lieutenant and decided to have some fun. "Are you saying my daughter is not attractive enough for you?"

"No, she is very cute," stumbled Lincoln.

"So you have been taking long glances at her then?" Luke shot back. He watched Lincoln shift uncomfortably in his chair.

"Not at all. I mean I only said hi to her. It's not like that. I don't know what it's like. I'm really sorry," finished Lincoln.

Luke let the boy breathe. He felt like a cat pawing at a grasshopper. If he was not careful, the Lieutenant might possibly bounce right out of his seat. He tried to calm the situation by saying, "You realize you do an awful lot of apologizing?'

"I do? I'm sorry," said Lincoln. Then, "Oh, I see what you mean. I only got this assignment because of my father. He is Captain of the Galatian. They wouldn't let us serve together, conflict of interest and all that. I don't have any training, but he pulled some strings."

Suddenly, Luke's elation deflated into pity. He felt bad for teasing the boy, something out of character for him. He felt it would be better to stick to business, but wanted to smooth things over first. He said, "If you want to see Mary again, come to me first. She is not to be alone with a young man yet."

Lincoln nodded. He tried to hide his smile by looking down at his computer monitor.

"I came here to discuss some problems that we are having in the fields."

"What problems, Mr. Umble?" asked Lt. Lincoln. "We are having problems all over the ship. If your son works close with Hux, he should know."

Luke thought about John's recent behavior. He could tell something was bothering his son, but the boy said nothing. If John knew of other problems besides the crops, he would have to have a long talk with him. For now, he had to concentrate on saving the harvest.

"It is the false sun. Whoever is in control of it is drying out our plants," explained Luke. "I tried to get them to change it. I told him we need more *night*. The deck supervisor said it is all controlled by computers up here."

"He's right, but if it is causing damage, he should have told us," said Lincoln.

"By my judgment, if it is not changed soon, it will cause a drought." Luke leaned in over Lincoln's desk. He almost whispered, "I don't know what it is like on the other levels, but a drought will destroy the harvest. What will we do for food?"

Lincoln matched Luke's low voice. "I probably shouldn't tell you this, but even if you bring in a full harvest, we would likely not have enough food for everyone."

"Mein Gott, what do you mean?" asked Luke. He felt his stomach drop to his knees.

"I know a little about farming and also, I read the reports," answered Lincoln. "All of the ships in this fleet were designed to carry ten thousand people each. Because of some bad decisions and some scared people, we only ended up with about seven thousand on board the Corinthian. The thing is, we only have around fourteen million square feet of usable land. The other ships use hydroponics and don't have the same issues with space. Fourteen million may sound like a lot of square feet, but under optimal conditions, according to recent surveys, that should produce enough food for two thousand people per year. See where I'm going with this?"

Luke did see and it almost crushed his heart. The *Englische* lied, that was his first feeling. They had to know of the inadequacies before letting anyone board. They had to know that in allowing the Amish to keep their traditional farming methods that they would starve. He knew nothing of hydroponics, but doubted that would even be enough to save them. It seemed that the *Englische* loaded them up into a floating coffin.

He moved back from Lincoln's desk as if he uncovered a rattlesnake in the wood pile. Luke knew it was not the young Lieutenant's fault. Still, it seemed like a good starting point for placing blame. It had to be someone's fault. Someone other than himself. He could not be responsible for delivering his family to such an end. Luke Umble was supposed to deliver them to salvation.

The entire walk back to his quarters, Luke wrestled with unpleasant thoughts. He could not get the dark things out of his head. He had a penchant for always imagining the worst scenario even when times were good. Now that he knew they were in trouble, he felt like he was losing control of his mind.

He opened the door to his deep space home, pulling hard on the once automatic panel. Annie stood in the middle of the room holding their lifeless baby Matthew. He shook his head with his eyes shut. That did not happen.

Closing his eyes did not make it easier. The idea of his family starving in space turned into them suffocating. If the *Englische* failed to plan for food, did it seem unreasonable that the life support could fail too? Once the oxygen stopped flowing through those tiny grates, there would be nothing they could do.

The false image twisted in his mind. Instead of a gaunt baby, Matthew now looked purple from lack of air. Luke stopped in the hall and pressed his head against his folded arms on the wall. He leaned for a moment trying to gather himself.

He said, "God, wipe these horrible visions from my mind's eye."

Luke did not pray. He did not ask. He said over and over that this was where God wanted him, despite what everyone else said. Luke did not want to admit that his father was right. He did not want to admit that maybe they should have stayed on Earth. Luke believed God wanted him to be the leader of his people on this voyage. Why, then, would He plague his servant with these images? Why would He save them from one fate only to beset them with another? Why would He challenge their faith in such a way?

Faith?

Did they still have faith out here amidst this vast nothingness? Could God reach them so far from Earth? Luke always believed his Lord was without end and without limits. At this moment, he started to doubt that. Never in his life did he have doubt like this. It took the threat of losing his family to push him so far. He always believed God's plan was the best, regardless of the physical outcome. He did not quite believe it now, especially imagining the suffering his wife, children and even his father might have to face.

He opened the door to his deep space home, pulling hard on the once automatic panel. Not a vision this time. Annie came from the kitchen. She must have seen the look on his face, the fear in his eyes. She came straight to him and they hugged. They had not hugged with such passion in a long time. Luke even wondered if they had that passion in them anymore.

For several minutes, they stood in each other's arms. Neither said a word. Eventually, Levi emerged from his room.

"Excuse me," said the old man. He must have thought he interrupted a private moment, guessed Luke.

"Would you like some?" Luke teased. He found the humor helped suppress the worry.

"Bah," Levi waved a hand. "I only came out of my room because I have a taste for cheese. Is there any of that horseradish bacon cheddar?"

Annie moved away from her husband. He could see her embarrassment from being caught at such behavior. She said, "Mr. Umble, you know we have not had that flavor of cheese on board. Your choices are white or yellow. I cannot say much more about their flavor than that."

Levi continued on to the kitchen. He said, "I know that. I am not going senile. Yet. That does not change the fact that I have a taste for that flavor. I look forward to Heaven. I expect the cheese buffet will be a mile long with fountains of honey. I do miss that sticky stuff."

Luke and Annie watched Levi rummage in the kitchen. He came back with a small block of yellow and a handful of crackers. Once he closed the door to his room, Annie asked, "Is there something you wanted to say, husband?"

It took a few minutes for Luke to recount his discussion with Lt. Lincoln. He purposely omitted the part about Mary. The information did not seem to frighten his wife. She had always been the stronger partner in their relationship.

"I want to grab John by the front of his shirt and shake him," said Luke. He sat down at the table.

"You will do no such thing. He is a young man and prone to make mistakes. We raised him in God's way. He is as stubborn as his father and his father before that, but he will come around," said Annie.

"But when? What more does he know about our situation? What worse could happen to us than starvation?" Luke had so many questions and no answers.

Annie stood behind her husband. She stroked his thinning hair while he fidgeted with his hat. She said, "I know the space between us on our mattress has grown wider these past few years. Long before all of this. The man I married seemed to wander off. I caught a glimpse of him on board this space ship. You showed me the strength of your beliefs over twenty years of marriage. Are you going to throw all of that away over one little problem?"

Luke tried to hold back his tears. How could he have forgotten how much he loved his wife? Her strength and character stirred long forgotten butterflies in his stomach. She was a beautiful woman that gave him five beautiful children. Maybe they would be dead soon, but he still had enough time to honor and love her how she deserved. The way she helped him figure out their problems made him smile. He squeaked out a slight chuckle, "It's not a little problem."

Annie draped her arms around his neck and kissed his teary cheek. She said, "I think we should talk with the whole family. None of us felt like you were very honest about this trip. Honesty may be the best approach going forward. The kids will be home from school soon."

******

The kids would be home soon. At least Mary and Katie would be. Eight-year-old Henry had other plans.

Back on Earth, Henry loved his animals. He used to run with dogs and chase the cats around the barn. He helped brush anybody's horse that he could. Unfortunately for the chickens, he even had the chore of gathering eggs. This did not usually end well for the eggs or chickens. The Umbles had a family joke that a dozen consisted of only eleven eggs.

Henry had yet to see a single animal on board the Corinthian. He half expected a space ship to have at least one cat slinking around the empty corridors. He had been promised repeatedly that he would be taken to see the animals, but always something interrupted those plans. He thought Mindi was nice enough, but she never took him.

"What good is a tour guide if she won't give a tour?" Henry asked one of his new friends at school.

Nice or not, Henry could tell there was something strange about Mindi. She promised him animals. He wanted animals. She did not come to the Umble quarters very often, but when she did, he asked. Instead of answering his question, she got that funny blank look on her face. He thought it was like she went somewhere to get an answer, but left her body behind.

Today, Henry planned to change that. If Mindi or any of the other *Englische* would not take him, he would find his own way. He had been assigned to a classroom on a different level than Katie to be with kids closer to his age. For that reason, he slipped away easily without either of his sisters noticing. Henry had no idea where they might keep the animals, but he had a whole day to search.

It seemed reasonable that there would be horses for working the fields. He did not think to ask his father if there were. As he headed toward the elevator, Henry thought about his father. He would be disappointed that his son was skipping school. Henry could not remember on which level his father worked. Instead of risking a chance encounter, the boy decided to go to a lower level.

Henry chose Level Eleven. He pushed the button and after a few seconds the doors opened again. It could have been the same hallway. Every level looked the same to Henry. It did not help that he felt no movement inside the elevator. He remembered being on an elevator once when he was maybe four years old. An experience like that left quite the impression on a young Amish boy. He could feel the difference between real gravity and artificial gravity, although his mind could not quite comprehend it.

One thing told him he was definitely on a different level. The temperature. It had to be at least ten degrees hotter on Level Eleven, he guessed. Henry had no way to tell the temperature other than he felt hot. Most of the levels seemed to have a constant cool breeze. Stepping out of the elevator, he could immediately feel the warm, sticky air. It did not seem to move, but rather hung around him like steam. Henry almost slipped on the moist floor. This did not seem normal.

Walking down the hall, the steam became thicker. The yellow wall lights caused the cloud to glow. Henry knew a field had to be at the end of this hall. Every floor except the bridge and engineering had a field. He continued forward blindly. Henry knew something like this would scare Katie and probably Mary too. She was sixteen now and pretended not to get scared, but Henry thought he could still scare her if he wanted to. Henry did not have time to be scared. He wanted to see some animals and nothing else mattered today.

The steam finally cleared. Henry expected to look out across a wheat field or maybe corn. Instead, he faced a wall of trees. Vines hung down from the branches and wide-leafed plants sprung up in between the trees. The whole place felt humid like after a summer rainstorm and everything looked wet. If he remembered his lessons correctly, this had to be a tropical rainforest.

"They're cutting back water consumption again."

Henry heard a voice, but could not see the man it belonged to. It came from somewhere inside the trees. He sounded *Englische*. A second man's voice, also hidden by lush greenness, responded.

"It's these Amish, I tell ya."

The way the man said *Amish* told Henry that these two definitely were not. Then the thick plants rustled near him. The men sounded upset with the Amish and he did not want to wait around to find out why. Instead of heading back down the hallway, Henry cut left, making a T from his original course. When he came to the first opening, he turned into the forest. The man-made path wound through the trees in countless curves. In only a few moments, Henry could only see green and hear nothing but dripping water as it tapped on the wide, thirsty leaves.

No one appeared to be following him, so he decided to sit and rest. The hot air made his breath feel heavy. Henry sat at the edge of the path on the lip where metal walkway surrendered to the earthen floor. He must have sat on some kind of trapdoor because it instantly gave way. Henry dropped through the floor and plopped into about six inches of water. The grate flipped closed above him. He got to his feet, but even on tip toes, he could not reach the way out.

In almost total darkness, Henry started to regret thinking his sisters would be scared. He could feel the water flowing around his shins. It made sense to him to follow the flow. Maybe it would lead to a way out, he hoped. As he walked, every so often, more grates would pop open, dumping surplus water down into this strange world. Henry assumed this was some kind of collection area for extra water. Maybe it came all the way down from the highest level.

Finally, Henry bumped into a wall. He guessed the water collection area stretched under the entire rain forest. He felt like he had been walking for a long time. Against the wall, he could hear the rush of water. Henry knelt and put a hand to the wall. The water rushed through filter screens at the base of the wall. He had no idea where it went from there.

"There has to be a way out of here," he said to himself. Henry kept running his hands along the wall, hoping to find a door of some kind. His fingers eventually felt a round metal circle. It seemed much larger than a doorknob, but not as big as a wheel on his old toy-wagon. He tried to turn it anyway. At first, it did not budge, but a second try got it to turn. He cranked it hard and what he thought was a door seemed to give. After a few more spins, the door swung away from him.

Henry fell out of the dark water tank into a brightly lit control room. Standing up, he saw gauges and dials labeled with words like *Reclaimed* and *Potable*. This had to be the control room for all of the ship's water he guessed. He did not have long to look as an angry looking *Englische* came toward him.

The man said, "What are you doing here?"

Henry ran. More than the fear of the angry worker, Henry did not want to have to answer to his father. He knew it was bad enough skipping school, but now he could be in real danger or real trouble. He had no idea which way led back to the elevators, but he kept turning corners and running.

A thick clear door blocked his path. It seemed to be made of the same material as the viewing windows he saw on their first day aboard the ship. It had a few words painted across its center: *Biology – Authorized Personnel Only.*

Henry had no other choice but to turn around. He bumped into some powder-blue coveralls. The inhabitant of the work uniform smiled down at him. Henry breathed a sigh of relief that it was not the man from the water control room. This *Englische* looked a lot like Mindi, but he could tell it was not her. She did not seem to recognize him either.

"I am Crewman G54. You may call me Sera. How can I help you?" she said.

"Um, Sera, I'm Henry. I was looking for some animals and I got lost." Henry did not know why he told her about the animals. His parents raised him to tell the truth, but he did not think that always applied to the *Englische.*

Sera got that faraway look in her eyes like Mindi or his teacher sometimes did. Henry really wanted to know where they went when they did that. When the almost creepy smile came back to her face, Sera said, "Please, follow me."

The crewman typed a code on the keypad next to the door. The clear panel slid into the wall and she led the way into the Biology department. Henry stepped through and the door immediately closed behind them. They were trapped in a small chamber. An intense red light flashed several times and jets of air and smoke struck him from above and below.

"Sterilization complete," said a computerized voice from a small speaker on the wall. A second door opened and Sera continued to lead the way.

Henry found himself in a perfectly white room. Soft light seemed to come from the ceiling and floor.

This place looked nothing like the rest of the dreary ship. It was all glass and plastic, almost no metal. In the places where he could see metal – a few tables and doors on the wall – it was stainless steel, not any of the dull brown he had grown used to.

"This is Biology. The department is on the outer hull of Level Eleven. If you wish to return to your quarters, I can direct you to the elevator. However, if you wish to see the animals, you will find them along this wall here." Sera pointed down the long hall that must have ran most of the length of the ship.

A myriad of cylinders stuck partially out of the wall as far as he could see. Henry moved close to examine the first row. He could not see inside the metallic cylinders, but they were cold to the touch. Each tube had a label with a seemingly random code followed by two names. On this, the first name sounded scientific: Canis Lupus Familiaris. This did not mean too much to Henry. The second name meant something more: Golden Retriever.

"A dog? You have a dog in this little container?" asked Henry. He felt some surprise, but mostly confusion.

"Of course," said Sera. She stopped, blank for a moment, then "Not actually a dog. That is the DNA base for the breed known as Golden Retriever. You will find seventy-eight point six percent of all Earth mammals, birds, insects and reptiles in this chamber, including over two hundred extinct species. You appear disappointed. Are these not the animals you wanted to see?"

Disappointed? Yes, Henry was disappointed. He wanted to see living, breathing animals. He wanted to pet furry creatures or even hold a squirming frog. He could not understand how the *Englische* fit all these animals into such small containers.

Before Henry could ask any other questions, the computer voice interrupted them, "Sterilization complete."

Mindi led his father and older brother into the Biology Department. Luke Umble came in saying, "I cannot stand to lose another child on this ship." He walked straight to his son and Henry feared the worst. Instead of a whipping, his father hugged him."

John cut their reunion short. He said, "Pa, what is this place?"

Luke looked around. Henry read his father's face and it looked like he had a better idea of this secret they discovered.

Luke said, "Mindi, would you please take Henry home? John and I have to talk to Ms. Huxtable."

Mindi agreed and took Henry by the hand. As they left, Sera said, "Goodbye, Henry."

******

"That is ungodly," exclaimed Luke. He had an idea of what Henry discovered, but Huxtable made it clear.

Hux finished wiping her hands and tossed the dirty ragged. It hung neatly on a knob protruding from an overhead pipe. She said, "How else do you think we would transport them? We barely have enough food and water for the humans. Did you think we would keep livestock on board too? Each ship has the same contingency of embryos and DNA samples."

Luke took off his own hat. Traversing the length of the ship and all the excitement left him a sweaty mess. He mopped his head and continued his conversation.

"Ms. Hux, that is the problem. We do not have enough food to feed even the humans," said Luke.

"What are you talking about?" she replied. John must have read the look of fear on her face. He placed an arm around her shoulder. This surprised Luke only slightly. He suspected his son had feelings for her. He did not realize how far those feelings had developed in such a short time.

Luke recounted his conversation with Lt. Lincoln for the second time. Then Hux shared her knowledge of the engineering problems that she previously told to John.

Not having any living animals on board made Luke wonder where they were getting things like milk and cheese from. It also explained things like the pouches of liquid eggs. His head swam with all of this new knowledge and a sense of betrayal. The failing crops seemed slightly less significant.

In an attempt to escape certain death, Luke put his faith in man and machine. He should have known that only God can be completely trusted. Only God never fails. Maybe his father was right. Maybe they left God back on that dying planet. Luke Umble could not and would not accept that there was no way to get back to Him.

Six

Deliverance

"I am going back to the captain," Luke said.

The looks on Hux and John's faces told him they were concerned. Of course they were, he told himself. Between the three of them, they knew enough to see that they were trapped with almost no alternatives. Neither of them tried to stop him as he turned to leave. The captain seemed like a volatile man. Confronting him about their situation would do no more harm than any other inconvenience they put before him.

Making his way along the dismal corridors, Luke recounted everything. He wanted Captain Nixon to know that he knew it all. Maybe, he even knew a few things the captain did not. He had to explain the crops were failing, at least on his level. He assumed it there had to be similar issues on each level of the ship, although he understood that different crops needed different amounts of light and water. Even if the crops were not failing, they did not have enough to feed everyone on the ship. Whatever synthetic food they had been using would be long gone before the crops could ever yield enough for them to survive.

Worse than that, they were running out of water. He knew the Amish faced difficult times in their past. For hundreds of years, since the beginning of their faith, they had been persecuted. The plain people lived through these times, they suffered through these times. Sometimes that meant without food or through a drought. Luke knew they could do it now. He knew they could make it for a short time without food. Maybe long enough to reach a suitable planet or rendezvous with another ship in the Adam Corp fleet.

Without water…

The visions came back to Luke. Why did his mind always show him the worst possibilities of every situation? Ghostly faces of his wife and children filled his head. The stretched, dry skin of his father's face overshadowed them all. The old man's mouth moved, but no sound came. Luke could read the lips; he did not need to hear the imagined voice to know it said, "Your fault."

Even in better times, Luke's mind worked like that. Some nights, he lay awake, his back toward his sleeping wife. He could not close his eyes without wondering if they would open in the morning. He had no reason to think he would die in his sleep. He stayed in perfect health and felt fine. Still, his restless mind kept him from peace. If he did not have dreadful thoughts of himself, it would be about one of his children, usually Katie.

Poor Katie. Riding up the elevator toward the bridge, Luke's thoughts turned to his daughter and her disease. He knew her struggles on this ship would only get worse. Even when they learned of her Muscular Dystrophy, Luke never asked why or blamed God. The same with these dark thoughts that often crowded his head. Luke saw it as an affliction of the enemy. As God worked in mysterious ways, Lucifer worked in secret. The enemy planted these thoughts in Luke's head and often, a simple prayer would bring light to his darkness. However, they thoughts eventually came back.

Now, the day dreams, or day nightmares, clung to Luke like shackled weights. He half-expected to hear them clanging on the walkway behind him. With all of the mental baggage he carried, they elevator should have crashed to the lowest level of the Corinthian.

The moment before the elevator door opened onto the bridge, Luke offered up a prayer. In this moment, Father, I give you my thanks for allowing me to find my way back to a strong, loving wife; for putting your shield around my children and giving me peace in a moment of crisis.

Peace.

The elevator stopped moving. Luke enjoyed a moment of silence and clarity. None of the dark thoughts hung on him, only a sense of purpose. The elevator doors opened.

Chaos.

The *Englische* ran about the bridge. Alarms beeped and blared. Captain Nixon stood in the middle of the bridge, towering over his desk. A busy young woman pushed past Luke, leaving a trail of papers behind her. The captain yelled orders.

"Hard starboard! No, starboard!"

Luke looked for some sanity in the room and found none. Even Lt. Lincoln ran like a madman. He scrambled from console to console, pushing the operators out of the way. He seemed to think he could do a better job at whatever needed doing.

"Get him out of here," demanded Captain Nixon.

It did not take much to figure out that the captain meant for someone to remove Luke from the bridge. Whatever was happening, Luke would not let it deter him from his mission. What could be more important than their food and water, he wondered. Lincoln started toward Luke.

"No, lieutenant. I need you at your post. Have one of the clones escort him. They're about useless for anything else," ordered the captain.

Clones? For an instant, Luke had no other thought than clones. Then he saw Mindi heading for him. Could Mindi be a clone, he asked himself. Before he could ask her, she gripped his upper arm with exceptional force. Her usual smile vacant, she moved them both toward the elevator.

"It's too late," shouted Lincoln.

At Lt. Lincoln's words, half of the crew members ran away from the large viewing windows. Lincoln ran toward them, so Luke pulled himself free of Mindi and followed the young man.

Outside the ship, Luke saw a magnificent painting of celestial beauty coupled with sheer horror. He did not understand exactly what happened before him. Massive chunks of ice or crystal spun out of a gassy cloud. Trails of small rocks and debris followed the larger objects, dragged along by their force of being.

Lincoln turned to him for an instant, "Comets. We never saw them coming, but I think we will miss them."

Looking out the window, the comets hurled in from the upper right of his view. Luke never witnessed a more awesome display of God's creation. The two largest comets could have easily been half the size of their ship. A collision with one of them could easily destroy the ship. All of their other worries of food and water would be irrelevant. Some of the tiniest debris bounced off the front of the ship. Ice crystals exploded into dust.

Luke followed the trail to his lower left. At the farthest edge of his view, he saw another object.

"Vas is das?" he asked. Lincoln did not appear to understand. He repeated, in English, "What is that?"

Now Lincoln saw it. He spun around and yelled at his captain, "It's the one of ours. She's course-corrected directly at us. Brace for imp…"

Before he could finish, the other space ship collided with them. As Luke fell into Lt. Lincoln, he saw the captain flip backwards over his desk. Then everything went black.

It took a minute for Luke to understand what happened. Apparently, the viewing windows were not completely impervious, so they had been equipped with blast shields. When the other ship hit them, the shields automatically closed. At the same time, the power went out on the bridge. Both things happening at the same time left them in total darkness. Luke stayed still on his hands and knees until emergency lighting brought the bridge back to some level of reality.

Lincoln sat up next to Luke. He appeared dazed, but otherwise unharmed. The young man stood and returned to duty, calling, "Status report."

Luke appreciated the boy's sense of responsibility. He allowed that maybe someone like this would be good for his Mary.

Mary!

Annie, the kids, his dad! Luke needed to get to his family. He needed to make sure they were safe. He said as much to Lt. Lincoln.

"The elevators will be shut down, standard procedure. We don't want anybody getting trapped or worse. There is a maintenance ladder. I'll have Mindi take you." He grabbed Mindi by her coverall strap. "Take Mr. Umble to his family. Do you know which ship hit us?"

Mindi paused with that blank expression that Luke knew so well. She said, "Negative. We are not back online yet. Mr. Umble, this way please."

Luke followed the woman in the powder blue jumpsuit. He tried to wrap his mind around so many things. Giant comets did not hit them, yet one of their own ships had. More than that, the *Englische* had clones running the ship. Were they all clones, he wondered. He guessed that only the ones in the coveralls were. The captain and Lt. Lincoln wore uniforms like most of the bridge personnel. They must be human. What's more, he wondered what Mindi meant by being *back online*. Were they somehow connected to the ships computers?

They stopped in front of the captain's desk. Mindi removed a slotted floor panel with one hand. Rubbing his arm from their earlier encounter, Luke marveled at her strength. The top rungs of a ladder led down into a dark, hungry-looking hole. If they ship had been alive, Luke thought now it was ready to eat him. That thought stopped him cold. *Father*, he prayed, *of all the dark and dreary that comes to my mind, I realize my faith is not so strong and I have many fears. I turn to You to allay those fears and ask that You share with me an ounce of the strength You gave Your Son. I would like to add, I never would have guessed we would end up in a space crash. I see You are making a point and You have my attention.*

Mindi started down the ladder. There must have been a motion sensor, because as she descended little white lights illuminated the tunnel. Luke followed the clone down the ladder. Right before he disappeared into the tunnel, Luke looked under the captain's desk. On the far side, he saw the unpleasant man still lying on the floor. His neck looked to be twisted in a very unnatural way.

******

Nick Lincoln could not understand why everyone started calling him captain. He knew the other ship hit them. He knew the bridge went into emergency lockdown. He tried to think what other relevant information he had.

The comets came out of nowhere. They were not on any charts or in any databases. Shouldn't those analytic geeks have spotted them? Apparently the gas cloud blocked the comets from the long range sensors. Once they started evasive maneuvers, he figured only chance could save them.

Lincoln called for a status report because he did not hear Captain Nixon call for one. Then he got Luke Umble off the bridge. The man needed to tend to his family, plus they did not need the extra distraction on the bridge right now.

The collision with the other ship shook the bridge. It knocked most people off their feet and apparently disabled some of the vital systems. Nick had to make sure life support still worked. As he moved from console to console, checking systems, the bridge crew started to refer to him as *Captain*. It did not make sense. He thought maybe people were in shock and saying the first thing that came to mind.

Finally, a junior analyst brought him a status report. The analyst said, "Ship's status, Captain."

"You know I'm only the Lieutenant, right?" said Nick. Maybe he thought the young lady was confused. They had never spoken before now; it could be a simple misunderstanding.

"Sir, the captain's dead. That makes you the captain," she answered.

Nick forgot the status report. Information about their condition and that of the other ship would have to wait. He maneuvered through the obstacle course that had once been the bridge. Two medics flanked the captain's body when Lincoln reached the desk. They already had a brace around the captain's neck. The heart monitor on his chest returned no readings.

I'm the captain now, thought Nick. He dropped back into the captain's chair for fear his knees would stop working. He had not wanted to assume the responsibility in such a way. In fact, he honestly had no interest in being captain. Now, sitting in Nixon's chair in front of the man's body, it felt like a punishment instead of a promotion. Nick swooned. How could he be responsible for seven thousand people? Of course, as the Corinthian's lieutenant, he was essentially already responsible. This made it somehow more real and he felt nowhere near capable.

As Nick watched the medics carry away Captain Nixon's body, he felt the paper still clutched in his right hand. *Why are we still using so much paper*, he mused. Somewhere, he understood, a printer still worked. Maybe the tablets were offline like the clones? He guessed the Wi-Fi had to be down too.

Nick unfolded the paper. Only a handful of casualties reported on the lower decks. Apparently the damage was mostly superficial. They did lose one of the zoological containment units. Fortunately, the majority of their biology departments were automated. Not many passengers were close to the outer hull during the collision.

The other ship did not fare as well according to the report. The Galatian did not evade the comets the way the Corinthian had. Captain Nixon ordered their ship to starboard, cutting away from the path of the comets. The second ship followed suit, but turned at a greater degree. The report said the second ship hit them head on, which forced it under the Corinthian. Nick imagined a giant letter T in space. The speed of the other ship pushed it downward and their bridge absorbed most of the continued impact. To top it all, the largest of the comets hit the tail of the second ship. The Galatian suffered critical structural damage.

Nick read the name of the ship again. The Galatian. His father captained the Galatian. Nick fought an urge to panic. He wanted to get to his father, but he was captain now. He could not abandon his post.

He called to the junior analyst, "What is the status of the Galatian?"

The young woman sorted through several more pages. She said, "The latest report has her adrift. No response from bridge crew and potential damage to the nuclear reactor."

"Where is she?"

"Directly beneath us, sir," answered the analyst.

Beneath – that was a relative term in space, thought Nick. He wanted badly to go to his father. It was at times like these that a young, inexperienced man needed a father most. Nick could not think straight. He had no idea who to turn the conn over to if he left the bridge. He looked at the junior analyst and said, "You're in charge until I get back."

******

The climb down the ladder took longer than Luke could have imagined. It gave him the time to think about his last words with God. He realized that he admitted his faith was weak. Then he wondered how long it had been that way and how weak it had become. Everything that led him to this moment, he thought he did from a righteous place. He stood tall with his chest inflated, stating that he delivered his family to salvation.

Not only had his faith suffered, but Luke now understood that he sinned. He had been proud for so long that it hung on him like a comfortable old coat. He dishonored his father, his wife and alienated his oldest son. Maybe the Earth fell on its last days, but he wondered if it was his place to take his family away from that fate. He reassured himself that if they stayed, they would all be dead. How was this any better, he asked himself. Would they not all be dead soon enough?

"No man shall know My plans."

Luke gripped the rungs of the ladder as if he had been welded to it. The voice came from below him. It sounded like Mindi, but not quite. He asked, "What did you say?"

"Nothing, Mr. Umble," she replied in her normal voice.

He could not see her face in the dim emergency lighting. It probably would not have done any good. When Mindi, or any of her crewmates, went blank, he could never read their expressions. He pressed her, "Only a moment ago, did you not speak of a plan?"

Mindi's voice came back to him a little distant. She must have continued climbing and he still did not move. She said, "No sir. I am not currently connected to the network. I am not authorized to make any plans or decisions on my own."

"But," Luke started to follow her down the ladder, "I heard you say something."

This time, Mindi stopped. He almost stepped on her uppermost hand. She said, "It is possible that I intercepted a wayward radio signal. You could have heard a broadcast from someone else. I have no memory of it."

It seemed logical, as much as Luke could make sense of it. He only learned that Mindi was some type of clone a short while ago. His son Henry would have hundreds of questions. He tried to anticipate some of them. From what he could gather, the clones must have had some type of internal antenna that connected them to the ship's network. Luke never had use for those things, but that did not mean he could not comprehend them. It made sense that if Mindi was not receiving her normal signal that she could pick up other signals. It seemed likely that there had to be a lot of radio traffic during an emergency like this.

Mindi opened a hatch. Luke saw a stenciled number eight in black paint on the hatch. They climbed out into the corridor only about fifteen feet from his family's quarters. How many times had he walked past this spot and never noticed the hatch, he wondered.

From there, Luke took the lead. He wanted to get to his family. He stepped through the already open door to find Annie sitting in the main room, clutching baby Matthew in his swaddling. Henry sprang from the couch and almost knocked him over with his hug. The flame of a single candle wiggled on the table in the middle of the room. Apparently the emergency lighting did not work in their quarters.

Luke dragged Henry back to the couch so he could sit with his wife. Levi emerged from his bedroom with a candle of his own. Before Luke could speak to Annie, his father had words for him.

"Is this the salvation you promised us?"

"*Daed*, this is not the time," said Annie.

"When is the time? When the devil himself walks the halls to deliver his personal invitation?" continued Levi.

Luke stood, eye to eye with his father. He said, "You're right."

Levi looked ready to launch another barrage. Then he stopped. His face changed slightly as he processed the words. Some of the wrinkles disappeared from the plowed field of his forehead.

"You are right," Luke said again. He looked to Annie and she seemed surprised. He noticed the hint of a smile. The candlelight reflected in her eyes, showing him that she supported him. She had always been the strong one in their relationship and she gave him courage. "Daed, I have been proud and blind. You said that we left God back on Earth. I am afraid that I have. God is everywhere in this unending universe, but my faith fell short infinitely. God did not leave me, I left him. I thought he wanted us to make this journey. I saw it as a pilgrimage. Now I see that fear replaced my faith. I was not ready to lose my family. I fled and hid my cowardice with pride."

Levi said nothing for a moment. His eyes appeared to tear over for only an instant. Then he said, "Bah! You are a good man. It is a father's blessing to see his son be a better man than him. You walk in the Lord's favor. It is not for our eyes to see His grand design. Name one man in the bible that did not have to suffer and sacrifice to receive God's true glory."

A twenty year old weight lifted off of Luke's shoulders. That one moment changed their entire relationship. Luke said, "Will you forgive me?"

"Only if you will forgive a stubborn old man."

The father and son hugged for the first time since Luke's mother passed. Over Levi's shoulder, Luke saw Annie looking hesitant to interrupt. He stepped back from his father to see her.

Annie said, "Are the girls not with you?"

"Dear Lord, they must still be at school," said Luke. "Mindi, will you please stay with my family. I can find my way to the classroom."

He did not wait for her to agree. Out in the hall, he found the hatch to the emergency ladder. Luckily Mindi left the door ajar or he might not have found it. When he made it to the classroom, he found Lt. Lincoln and two other men attempting to pry open the door.

"It's jammed. I can hear some of the kids crying. I think they're alright, but probably pretty scared," explained the Lieutenant.

Luke remembered the hydraulic system from the doors in their quarters. Obviously it was not electronic. He pointed it out to Lincoln and the young man went to work. With a lot less effort than they previously used, the Lieutenant managed to disable the hydraulics. Then the door slid open with ease. Overly-excited children scampered out for their own quarters.

Inside the classroom, a few students remained behind with the teacher. Luke found Mary sitting on the floor next to Katie's wheelchair. The Lieutenant went to a young boy that had to be related to him.

"I told you he would come," Katie said to Mary. "He always comes back."

******

Several weeks passed. The *Englische* crews worked tirelessly to repair the ship. John did his part to help, but made it a point to have dinner with his family each night. The engineer, Hux, came with him.

"Most of the ship's controls are still offline," John said. Luke could see the worry and exhaustion in his son's eyes. "The crews are going section by section. The bulkheads are sealed until each room is cleared."

The *crews* were groups of volunteers, some headed by the *Englische*. Luke had his own crew working down on Level Ten. Where they could be spared, the clones, like Mindi, instructed the Amish men. The collision with the Galatian caused more damage than they first thought. The crews had a lot of clean up and many Amish learned how to do basic electrical repair.

Hux picked up where John stopped. Luke had more than one conversation with his wife as to how close John and Hux had become. The curly-haired engineer said, "We have not been able to contact the Galatian either. Right now, we are both drifting. The Galatian is dark."

Mary caught her breath. Luke looked down the table at his oldest daughter. She seemed like she might cry. He said, "What troubles you child?"

"Nick…I mean, Lt. Lincoln's father was captain of the other ship. He told me they don't think anybody survived," said Mary. Then she did start crying. Annie left her plate half full of food and took Mary into her bedroom.

No one spoke until they left the room. Luke watched his wife's shoulders as the two women walked away from him. It amazed him how much Annie could bear. She put up with him for all this time, he mused. Since the men stopped working the fields, some of the women took their place, trying to salvage what crops they could. With so many of the automated systems broken, they had no control of water or artificial light.

Annie, on the other hand, took charge in the kitchen. In the true Amish way, all of the families pooled the last of their supplies. Annie's group turned scraps into meals. They did not have loaves or fish, but she managed to feed whoever asked. Luke came home after a shift clearing debris to find a soup line of grateful people in his corridor. Mary helped her mother and the other women with cooking, while Levi and Katie ladled soup into bowls. Henry paced up and down the hall, rationing water to thirsty Amish and *Englische* alike. After a day of hard work for all of them, the whole family sat down together.

His wife did not cry in front of him, but Luke suspected Annie and Mary let out their frustrations in private. While they sat in Mary's room, the rest of the family continued their meal.

"If the controls are, as you say, offline, how does one steer the vessel?" Luke asked Hux.

"That's the problem," said Hux between spoonfulls. "The pilots can read some of the instruments. They can tell that we are drifting off course."

"Way off course and there are no other ships in sight. Mindi also told me that long range communications are gone," John added.

"Until they get the guidance controls back, we can't restart the VASIMR engine. There is no chance of calling for help. We are completely alone," she said.

Levi corrected, "We are adrift, but not alone."

"Amen," added Luke.

******

Mindi startled Luke at the beginning of his third shift that week. As different areas were cleared, the shifts were cut back. Instead of seven days, they were down to four. Energy had to be conserved in order to save food supplies. Annie miraculously managed to keep people fed, but the portions and varieties started to shrink.

As Luke entered the damaged hall, Mindi went blank. She had not done this since before the crash and it surprised him. Over the past weeks, he got used to the idea of her and the other crewmembers being clones. He had not decided what that meant to him. For the most part, he thought of them as normal people. One night, his father wanted to debate whether they had souls.

"If they have no souls, then they are no creation of the Father. It is not for me to decide, but I do not think they should be eating of our food supply," argued Levi.

The debate ended when Hux explained that the clones got their nutrition from a liquid chemical compound that fed not only their biological being, but also their internal electronics. Apparently, the hardware in their brain needed special fluids. Luke still wondered if they had souls, but it could wait. One brief talk with Mindi revealed that while they were all cloned from the same source, the computer components embedded in their brains technically made the crew members cyborgs. Mindi preferred to be called a clone because it sounded more pleasant to her.

When Mindi finally went back *online*, she must have had a lot of information to collect from the ship, thought Luke. She stood frozen for three minutes – longer than he had ever seen. Usually, one of the clones would blank for a moment or two, maybe thirty seconds. Then her lips started moving. No sound came with the movement.

Henry came to work with Luke. The sight of the motionless Mindi caught his attention.

"What's happening, Pa?"

"I do not know, son," answered Luke.

Then he heard Mindi's voice, quiet, like an August breeze grazing the top of a wheat field. He put his ear close to her mouth. It seemed a little inappropriate to be so close, but he thought she might be giving instructions or warning of danger. What he heard there gave him goose bumps and watered his eyes. He did not cry, but his eyes and cheeks showed otherwise.

"If I did not know better," he said to his son, "she is speaking in tongues."

"Like the Holy Spirit?" asked Henry.

Luke took Henry by the shoulder and pulled him to his knees. He said, "I do not know what manner of supernatural this is, but I think it best we pray." The two other Amish men behind him, Shipman and Laitinen, followed his actions.

Henry squeezed his eyes tight and laced his fingers. Luke could hear him reciting the Lord's Prayer.

"Father," said Luke, "I feel Your presence and give thanks that Your hand is on your people at this hour. I ask that we draw strength from Your guidance and hope from Your patience. I am Your willing servant and submit to Your will. Whatever may come, please fulfill Your promise to my family and all of Your people on board. For that, may all the honor and glory be Yours."

Mindi stopped mumbling when Luke finished his prayer. She blinked a couple times. "I am back online," she said. "What are you doing on the floor?"

"Praying," answered Henry.

"Your belief in God is curious," she said. Mindi bent to Henry's height and smiled. "I have access to a database of world religions. I think I will review the material. Sometimes, I feel like I should believe in something. My programming supervisor repeatedly assures me that it is not necessary."

Luke shuffled his son's hair. He said, "Maybe you should join us for our next church meeting. Belief is a powerful thing. When you feel alone or different, it can truly help." He could not decide how far to take this conversation. It may be best to leave the discussion of a clone's faith for a better time, he concluded.

Henry kept going, however. "What were those words you were saying?"

"I said nothing. There is no audible dialogue associated with my reboot process."

******

Nick Lincoln experienced a similar situation with the clones on the bridge.

"This would be a lot easier if *they* were back online." Lincoln nodded to the clone nearest him.

The junior analyst nodded in agreement. She said, "From what we can tell, the gas cloud stretches about six hundred thousand miles and we are still drifting toward it."

"And it wasn't on any of the charts?"

"Correct, sir. We are not sure what will happen once we pass through either," she finished.

The Lieutenant had no idea what to do. He never really got along with the late Captain Nixon, so he tried to imagine what his father might do. Thinking of his father and the Galatian hurt. He could not believe they were gone. He steeled himself. Mourning would have to wait.

All at once, the eight clones on the bridge froze and began speaking what sounded like gibberish. Nick looked from the junior analyst to the clones. Everyone stopped working and listened. The words made no sense, but it stirred something in his gut.

Or maybe it was his soul.

Spending time with Mary Umble made him think about his own Christianity. He believed in God, but had no real religious practices. His father raised him in a military fashion, but they did not frequent church. Nick liked the time he spent with the Umbles and other Amish. It got him thinking about his own beliefs. Right now, the chattering clones felt more like a spiritual experience than a technical glitch.

The instant the clones stopped speaking and came back online, one of the navigators yelled, "Something is coming out of the cloud!"

Lincoln ran toward the viewing window. Through the green-blue swirls of the gas cloud, he saw a massive white light.

"Is it the Galatian?" Nick thought it might be an explosion on the other ship. He knew the answer. The Galatian had fallen behind them and would likely be drifting away from the cloud. This was something else.

The object dwarfed his ship. It had no definite shape other than being longer than it was high. As it came out of the cloud, it grew in intensity. Nick could not see any individual lights. The thing glowed from the inside. He had to shield his eyes. Looking back onto the bridge, he saw everyone else covering their faces. The light turned everything white on board with sharp black shadows that cut across the room.

Lt. Lincoln could not look back at the object. His last guess had it moving straight toward them.

******

Once Mindi finished talking with Henry, Luke and his friends went to work. The three Amish lifted several ceiling panels that had fallen. Wires hung down over their heads and sparked when Laitinen bumped into a dangling cluster.

"The next section is a maintenance airlock," explained Mindi. "Nothing is supposed to be stored in an airlock, so we should be able to move through to the next area."

"Sounds like an easy day," said Luke as he hit the button to open the door.

The rush of air when the door opened pulled Luke forward. Air blew past him. He dropped to his knees, unable to stand with the pressure. He could see air almost liquefy, like a cloudy vapor, as it vented out of a narrow crack. The airlock door looked stuck open, but only by an inch.

"You have to get out of there," shouted Mindi.

Luke regained his balance. The atmosphere tearing into space roared around him. He had to raise his voice for Mindi to hear him. "Should we not seal this door?"

She called back, "We can lock the airlock from here." Although she was only a few feet away, her voice seemed to come from across one of his wide fields like a call for dinner after a day of plowing.

Luke looked around him. He could see the brown metal plates vibrating under the force. The door opposite from him looked sealed, but he could see the rubber around the frame starting to bulge. He believed that closing the inner door would not save them. This leak would continue to weaken the entire airlock. If he did nothing, it could mean more damage to the ship.

"Shipman, find me some rope," he ordered. Luke acted in the moment, his ego forgotten. He had to fix this because he was the one here at this moment. It had nothing to do with status or pride. Then he called to his son, "Henry, come here."

The boy slowly crawled to his father. His eyes kept darting to the lethal crack. Luke pulled Henry up from the floor and wrapped him in a fierce hug. He whispered instructions in his ear and then pushed the boy away from him. Henry ran from the airlock.

******

Red lights started flashing in every area of engineering. After the third false alarm, Hux disabled the audible alert. She could not take the bleating any longer as the alerts cycled through random electrical shorts.

Years of experience could not keep her from checking the system log though. As with the previous miscues, she expected to see another false entry. The reading on her monitor scared her this time.

"This is bad," she said loud enough for John to hear her. He stuck close by her. She liked that. Since the crash with the Galatian, he became the one she counted on most on Level Twelve. Some of the other more experienced engineers folded under the pressure. Maybe John was a few years younger than her, but he was more of a man than any she had ever known.

"What is it?" he asked.

Hux did not have time to explain it. She gave him the short version. "There is a hull breach. We're venting atmosphere. It's going to put the engine in a recycle mode if we don't shut everything down."

John followed her along the narrow catwalk. She grabbed the ladder and, foregoing safety for speed, slid down the outside. It took John a moment longer as he climbed down each rung. An instant later, he was by her side at the main console. She began tapping icons on the touch screen.

"What can I do?" asked John.

What can I do? Always sweet and eager, she thought. This boy came into *her* engine room and inserted himself from the first day on board. It impressed her and distracted her. Hux never thought about anything except schematics and optimizations, until John. When she met him, she could think of little else but him. He remained a perfect gentleman. Their relationship never developed into anything more than a working one. In a way, that was perfect for Hux. She could maintain her engine and be in his company. At this moment, their arrangement seemed lacking. She realized something in her haste. His helpfulness flustered her and she had to do something about it.

Hux said, "Two things. I need you to reset the artificial gravity controls. We're going to put the ship in a spin to trick the computer. I can't stop the auto-recycle."

John started to move, then turned back toward her. He asked, "What's the other thing?"

"This," she said. Hux grabbed the sides of his sweaty face and kissed him. She could not bring herself to say the words. She never said it to any other man, she never had cause to. She hoped her eyes told him *I love you.*

******

The light streaming in through the bridge windows continued to grow brighter. Lt. Lincoln could feel the temperature increasing. Through the glare, he watched fellow crew members collapse around him. The junior analyst fell at his feet. Nick did not think it was too hot, but he could think of no other reason people were fainting. He hoped they were only fainting.

He could barely see the face of the young woman as he knelt to check on her. Then everything went dark. Nick tried to look out the window. He wanted to know if the light was gone, but he could only see green spots in front of his eyes. It took a long minute for his eyes to adjust enough to see anything.

Outside, the object now looked completely black. It looked like a ship, but far bigger than anything Nick could have imagined. More than a spaceship, it looked, to him, like a block of obsidian. As bright as it had been moments ago, the ship looked impossibly black. No light escaped from it, except that it seemed to reflect the distant stars. If he had not seen the light from it, had not been so close, Nick swore he would have never known it was there.

He moved from the floor. The Lieutenant surveyed the bridge and saw no other movement. Whatever that ship did to the people on the bridge, it had not affected him. He wanted to scan the ship. He needed to know what was inside it. Or who.

Accessing the nearest console, he thankfully had the use of short range scans. After the combination burst of sonar and radar, Lincoln checked the readings. Maybe, he thought, the short range system was not working either. As far as his instruments were concerned, there was nothing out there between him and the gas cloud.

Before he could recheck his readings, Nick saw a burst of light come from the strange ship. It came directly toward the bridge. Nick ran away from the viewing window. He knew he could not make it to the emergency ladder before it hit. Whoever or whatever controlled that ship, he guessed they were not friendly since they fired a weapon at him. He ducked behind a row of computers a second before the impact.

Nothing happened.

Nick looked up from his hiding spot. The white ball of light floated outside the window. He thought it looked like a person. The white light emanating from inside the object made it impossible to tell for certain. As he watched, this new object passed through the two-foot thick synthetic glass as if it was not there. Again, Nick thought it resembled a person. It seemed to walk down the center aisle of the bridge, but it never touched the floor.

"Hello," said the Lieutenant. Did he really expect a response? The being, he assumed it was a being, turned toward him. It made no gestures. It did not appear to try to communicate at all. Lincoln watched as it stopped in front of the main navigation panel. It extended what could have been an arm. A narrow stream of light poured out of the appendage causing the computer screen to wildly channel through hundreds of course sequences.

When the being completed its task, it disappeared back to its ship as suddenly as it arrived.

＊＊＊＊＊＊

Shipman and Laitinen tied the rope around Luke's waist, despite Mindi's protests. They temporarily closed the inner door. Luke could breathe easy and hear the clone perfectly.

"You cannot go back out there. It is true you will have oxygen from the ship, but the exposure could kill you," she stated.

"I have a feeling that if I don't fix it, the leak could kill us all. My life is a small sacrifice," said Luke. He desperately needed to believe that. For too long, he lived in fear of death and lied to himself about it. Had his faith been truly as strong as he presented to the world, he might never have made the choices that brought them to this point.

Now that he faced the real possibility of death, he only felt peace. He discovered his own faults and gave them up to God. The only that mattered was saving the ship. At least, Henry had not heard his discussion with Mindi. He knew Annie and his father would understand, but he did not know if the kids would.

Finally, Henry returned. He completed his father's task by presenting Levi's hammer.

Who brings a hammer on a spaceship, Luke asked himself again. Looking at his son holding the hammer up to him, he thought of God as the master of the *If*. If Levi never brought the hammer, he would not be able to help the ship at this moment. But, *if* he never got on the ship, where would he be? He understood that only God had all the answers to the *if* questions. Only He could set events in motion hours, days, years or centuries before His plan came to fruition. Luke knew all he could do was have faith and know that God always kept his promises.

"Ready," said Luke.

Shipman and Laitinen braced themselves at the end of the hall and pulled the rope tight. Henry grabbed the end, even though he did not know the plan. Luke knew Mindi did not want to re-open the door, but he watched her reluctantly do it. The ripping wind started immediately. Inside the airlock, Luke could see ice forming around the outer door. The yellow lights hidden behind the wall plates popped and winked out.

Luke crawled forward. The metal floor grew colder as he neared the door. He could feel the power of the open door straining against the rope. Not only did space pull the atmosphere out of the ship, he could feel it stealing from his lungs. Luke found the cause of the problem. A metal rod, that matched nothing else around, wedged perfectly to keep the outer door from closing.

If he had to guess, Luke thought they were near the area where the Galatian struck their ship. He had no real way to know, but suspected the airlock burst open during the crash. This stray piece of debris must be a gift from the lost ship. He told himself that it did not matter where it came from; it only mattered that he removed it.

He raised the hammer to strike at the rod, then everything shifted. It felt as if gravity itself ceased. One moment, he knelt on the floor and then he fell against the door. Luke guessed the ship was somehow tumbling in space. Early on, the *Englische* technicians explained that the artificial gravity would hold them to the floor no matter which way it turned. Now, it felt like the artificial gravity stopped working or changed its mind how it wanted to work. Luke could not worry about that. He had to clear the door. Kneeling on it, he began to pound and he hoped the door would not open with each hit.

WANG.

Luke felt his arms growing weaker.

CLANG.

The lack of oxygen caused his eyes to go blurry.

STRUNG, then HISS.

The door slid closed. Looking through the small portal in the middle of the door, Luke saw the steel rod spin off into space. He tumbled to his side, gasping for air. His fingers barely moved, feeling like they suffered from a deep-winter frostbite. He dropped the hammer and slowly closed his eyes. Before he faded away, he thought he saw the glowing white figure of a person outside the circular window.

******

Annie watched her latest batch of soup begin to rise out of the pot. It climbed up the side and began dripping toward the wall in a bizarre display. Then everything in the kitchen began to shift. At first, Annie tried to grab bowl and keep them from slipping. Then something else occurred to her.

"Matthew's crib," she ordered.

Mary needed no other explanation. She dashed to the bedroom to keep the baby from falling.

Annie turned to Levi and Katie in the middle of the room. Her daughter's wheelchair rolled uncontrollably. Levi did not react in time. Annie watched her daughter roll out the open door of their quarters. She feared how Katie's weakened body would handle the impact.

By the time Annie slid down the floor and made it to the door, she looked out to see what could have been a human bathed in white light holding the back of Katie's wheelchair. The being adjusted the chair safely and then floated down the corridor.

******

Hux watched the water churn behind the massive containment wall. She said a small prayer for the glass to hold at the same moment that it began to crack. Then she thought she saw someone swimming inside the huge tank. The being shone with an incredible light that made the water sparkle. The glass cracked again and a stream of water spewed out and then stopped. Somehow, the stranger held in the water. Hux knew she had no time for anything else.

John finished adjusting the gravity controls. Until they completed the full rotation, they would have to climb to get out of the engine room. She called to him, "We have to go now!"

The chief engineer started climbing and saw John right behind her. She did not know how long the containment wall would hold. The engine would be lost, but they could seal the bulkhead and keep the rest of the level from flooding. Other engineers and technicians scrambled past. John looked back to see that the engine room was clear. He hugged her and the feeling of his arms comforted her. Then he punched the button to close the doors, but they did not close.

Hux looked back into the engine room below her. She could no longer see the white being in the water tank. She watched the glass burst and water sprayed out into her domain. Everything she knew and loved, with the exception of John, would be gone. The doors had to be closed though. If the water made it out, it could get into ventilation and destroy the life support system. She hit the button again and still nothing.

"I'll have to close them manually," John said.

She could not let her first love go into something he would not come back from. Hux said, "It's my engine room. I'll do it."

John surprised her. He said, "I love you, but you're crazy. There's no way you can close all the valves before you run out of breath."

A bittersweet thought passed through her head. She had trained him well. He must have remembered there were four valves that needed to be closed to release the hydraulics. She said, "Fine. You do two and I'll do two."

This time, John kissed her. Love felt different that duty and responsibility – things she had known all her life. Love felt good and despite what they were about to do, it felt safe. They clasped hands and jumped through the bulkhead door. They splashed into the water and it was unexpectedly warm.

Hux watched John take a deep breath and disappear below the surface. She followed him. They swam past control consoles and into the narrow space where she first realized she had feelings for him. The hydraulic control area was a tight fit under normal circumstances. Swimming in water made the access a little easier and Hux allowed herself the hope of being able to swim back to the doors before they closed.

As fast as she could, Hux spun two of the valves. Bubbles eeked out of the joint where the wheel connected to the pipe. She felt the pressure on her lungs and needed to get back to the surface. She checked to see if John had finished. He let go of the last valve and pointed upward. Hux started to swim. She looked back, but he was not behind her. Desperately out of air, she swam back to her new love.

John's suspender strap somehow twisted around one of the valves and he could not get free. Hux fumbled in her pocket for her utility laser. She cut the suspender. It seemed strange that the laser made smoke underwater. John started to go limp and she pulled at John. Hux managed to get him through the narrow opening. All they had to do was swim up to the door. She could see the opening through the crystal clear, purified water. It wavered like a funhouse mirror, but the result of their efforts had not been realized yet. If they could swim fast enough, they could make it. John was not swimming though.

Hux could barely move and carry his body at the same time. With each stroke, she knew she had to be only a few feet from the surface. Through the shimmering water, she watched the door close. She had two thoughts. First, she knew before they jumped into the water that they would never make it out. Secondly, they had saved the ship.

The engineer and the Amish boy splashed to the surface. A small pocket of air remained. Hux grabbed a pipe to hold them above the water. She kissed John twice, almost like a life-saving maneuver. He sputtered and opened his eyes. The water lapped against their chins as they kissed one last time.

******

Lt. Nick Lincoln could do nothing but watch. More of those white-light beings rose from the Corinthian. The beings must have been all over the ship. He watched them sail back to their ship and then the unbelievably big vessel slipped back into the gas cloud.

As soon as the visitors disappeared, the people on the bridge awoke. Lincoln wondered how many of his crew witnessed the encounter. Like the people, the ship seemed to wake up too. Systems that had been offline since the crash beeped and chirped.

The junior analyst gathered herself and checked the nearest console for a status report like a well-trained officer. Nick had not asked for one. Words seemed insufficient at the moment. Besides, he had a feeling that everything would be fine.

"Sir," she said, "we are moving on impulse. There is no response from engineering and the VASIMR engine is still offline. However, we have a new course."

It did not surprise him that navigation was back online. He would personally go down to engineering, but first, he asked, "To where?"

"Into the nebula," she said.

Somehow, Nick expected that. The visitor obviously reprogrammed their navigation to take them directly into the giant gas cloud.

"According to our charts, there is nothing in there," continued the analyst.

"Don't be so sure," said Lincoln.

******

Luke opened his eyes. The dull brown ceiling that had become his life greeted him with indifference. He lay in an unfamiliar cot. He assumed Shipman and Laitinen carried him to the ship's hospital. He had never been in it, but knew they had one. He swung his bare feet to the floor. He did not feel the usual cool air. He hoped the climate controls had not failed.

Leaving his private room, Luke stumbled through a lab. His full strength definitely had not returned. He squeezed his fists and leaned against a counter for support. At least he had all his fingers, he noted.

A man that must have been the doctor said, "Mr. Umble, you should not be out of bed yet."

Luke ignored him. He had an urge to make sure the ship was safe. He needed to know and then he needed to see his family. The door slid open and he stepped out of the hospital.

A warm breeze and bright sunlight greeted him. Luke did not understand where he was. As far as he could see, lush greenery surrounded him. Off to his left, he could see the Corinthian resting on its huge landing gear. Amish men and women worked to unload supplies and erect small metal buildings like the one behind him.

He could see fruit hanging from nearby trees and birds cutting across the sky. Faint wisps of green clouds sailed on the breeze. This place looked like paradise – like Eden as he imagined it when reading his Bible. Somehow they found a planet. Somehow they survived.

Then Henry ran past him, chasing something that looked like a cross between a pig and a dog. Obviously, this place had its own unique species. Luke laughed at his son's playfulness. It made him happy to have a place for children to run.

Annie walked from around the corner with Matthew in her arms, followed by Mary holding hands with Lt. Lincoln. Further behind them, Levi sat on a bench with Katie, her empty wheel chair lay carelessly on its side. On the table in front of them, Luke saw a delectable feast picked from the glorious trees.

"There you are," said Annie with a kiss.

Katie smiled at her father from a distance when she heard her mother. She said, "You always come back."

"This place is miraculous," said Luke. He had so much to see and so many questions to ask.

Before he could speak again, a hand tapped him on the shoulder. He turned to see John standing with Chief Engineer Huxtable. His oldest son hugged him. They had not hugged like that in a long time. It brought a tear to Luke's eye.

John stepped back and waved his arm like he was presenting this new world to his father. John said, "Welcome home."